TO EVERYTHING A SEASON

Ian Searle

Copyright © 2023 Ian Searle

All rights reserved. No part of this publication may be reproduced or transmitted in any form or by any means, electronic or mechanical including photocopying, recording or any information storage or retrieval system, without prior permission in writing from the publishers.

The right of Ian Searle to be identified as the author of this work has been asserted by him in accordance with the Copyright, Designs and Patents Act 1988

First published in the United Kingdom in 2023 by
The Cloister House Press

ISBN 978-1-913460-68-6

To Everything a Season

Part one

"University?"

Daniel Cobden stared at the visitor in surprise and shock. When Mr Richardson, Ralph's Headmaster, had written to suggest he might call and discuss Daniel's son's future, Daniel had been puzzled. Ever since Ralph had won the scholarship he appeared to have been doing well. His termly reports all said he was hard-working and a very able pupil. Daniel's wife, Mary, was equally puzzled. Ralph was nearly seventeen, a good-looking boy, six inches taller than his father.

Ralph was used to helping on the farm. In term time, as soon as the school bus had dropped him at the end of the lane, he would head home, drink the cup of tea his mother gave him, change into his working clothes, and spend the remaining daylight hours on the farm. It was a routine he did not particularly enjoy, but while he had never questioned. His true love was his schoolwork, something neither of his parents could fully understand, although his mother was sympathetic and supportive. Once his work on the farm was done, and the three of them had eaten a large meal, and spent half an hour with the Bible, followed by a short prayer, Ralph would take himself off to his bedroom to do his homework, often reading until after midnight by the light of an oil lamp, since there was no electricity in the house. Now he had begun his sixth form work he had a lot of reading to do.

His father had been opposed to the suggestion that his son should spend two years in the sixth form, a time when Daniel had expected him to be working on the farm, but he had been persuaded by Mary that this was the right thing to do. Now, it seemed, Mr Richardson was suggesting a further delay.

"How long will that take?" Daniel asked. "And what use would it be? We can't afford it, anyway. Ralph's place is here. He will take over this farm, and I need him now. I don't even know why he's bothering with the Higher School Certificate. It's hard work here, you know. I need the help. Why does he need all this education? What good are Higher School Certificate in English or History going to do him here?"

Mr Richardson had heard much of this before. He pushed aside the plate on which Mary had handed him a generous portion of her fruit cake, looked at her for moral support, and tried to argue the case.

The three of them were sitting around the table in the parlour. It smelled vaguely musty, with overtones of Mansion Polish. It was only used on rare occasions for special visitors. The table was covered by a thick cloth. A large, Victorian sideboard gleamed from Mary's vigorous polishings. The teacher gathered his thoughts as the long case clock in the corner ticked in the otherwise silent room. He felt claustrophobic in the gloom. He had been forced to bend his head to enter, and to remain bent to avoid the dark beams. The ceiling, lit by the dull daylight from the small window, was uneven, like the sea. He wondered if the bedroom above sloped.

"Mr Cobden," he said at last, "are you sure Ralph wants to be a farmer?"

"Wants to be?" This was clearly a new idea for Daniel. "Wants to be?" he repeated, "What has wants to do with it? He's my son. This is his inheritance. It's his duty, what he was born for."

"Doesn't Ralph have a say in this?"

The farmer looked at him. His curiosity had given way to hostility. This man, educated, something of a toff, was challenging some of Daniel's basic beliefs.

"Have you ever asked Ralph what he wants?" Mr Richardson prodded him. Daniel was beginning to feel like his bull, Caesar, being poked with a cattle prod.

"What Ralph wants is neither here nor there," he declared. "And it's none of your business, either. He will come to work with me and then he'll take over. That's that."

"Daniel," Mary spoke to calm the situation. "Mr Richardson has a point. We should ask Ralph how he feels."

"You always were soft with the boy," her husband replied. "You're not agreeing, are you?"

"We both love our son," said Mary, "but surely we want him to be happy?"

"He has to do his duty," said Daniel, his jaw jutting with determination.

There was a minute's silence, filled by the ticking of the clock.

Next door, Ralph sat in the farm kitchen, close to the parlour door which he had contrived to leave slightly ajar. He sensed his future was at stake, and he was very aware of his father's plans for him. Secretly, he was determined that one day he would have to confront Daniel. He did not as yet have the courage. The idea of university was little more than a dream, but it might offer him the hope of escape. He trusted his teachers. The first obstacle was to remain at school long enough to get the required grades. State and County Scholarships were available, he knew.

"Forgive me if you think I am intruding into your personal affairs," Mr Richardson was saying," but you seem to be saying you need Ralph to work on the farm. It is already difficult for him to keep up sometimes."

"I can't do all the work on my own," said Daniel. "My wife helps, of course. She looks after a lot of the livestock and helps with the milking, but some of the heavy work needs a man. I have to wait until Ralph gets home some nights."

The teacher nodded. "Couldn't you take on a worker, even part-time?"

A look of incredulity met this suggestion.

"There's no way we could afford another hand," Daniel said flatly.

Without pausing to reflect, Mr Richardson replied, "Are you saying Ralph is cheap labour? Do you pay him for his work?"

"That's none of your business!" Daniel was angry at the implication that he was exploiting his own son "Ralph works as much as he can, but the farm has to support all three of us. He's never gone short in all his life."

No, thought the teacher, but he's never had any money to play with.

There was another silence.

"Well," said Mr Richardson, "we still haven't agreed on the idea of a possible university career."

"And you haven't said how long all this would take."

"Ah, no, you're right," said Mr Richardson, happy to concede the point and so get a more sympathetic hearing. "All would depend on his performance in the Higher School Certificate. I don't know if you could allow him a little more time to study. That would help. We think your son is quite gifted. He could well do well enough to guarantee a scholarship."

"Did you hear that, Daniel? Ralph, gifted!" Mary was bursting with pride. Her husband did not reply.

"How long?" he asked.

"Assuming he gets the right results and then be accepted, the degree course would take three years."

"Three years! And where would this be?"

"It could be anywhere, but we're hoping he can get into Oxbridge."

"Where's Oxbridge?"

"I mean Oxford or Cambridge."

"And he would have to live away from home? For three years?"

Mr Richardson nodded. "If he can do it," he said, "it will be a wonderful achievement. Only one percent of the population have a degree."

The farmer looked at him. "There's no way I can manage another five years," he said. "We aren't getting any younger."

"He will be liable for his National Service first, in any case. You'll have to cope without him then for two years."

"Oh no," the farmer said, as though playing a trump card. "He's exempt as a farm worker."

Outside, listening intently, Ralph was thinking hard. The mention of National Service set off another train of thought.

"You don't need to decide here and now," said the teacher. "Maybe you need to think about it and decide what is in your son's best interests. I would urge you to talk to him. He's a bright young man but if his heart isn't in it, he might not make much of a farmer. Have you thought of that?"

He stood, banging his head on a beam.

"Thank you for talking to me," he said.

In the kitchen Ralph slid quickly to the far end of the bench as his teacher came in.

"I'll see you on Monday, Ralph," he said. "Come to my office after assembly."

"Yes, sir," Ralph said, surprised by the use of his first name and Mr Richardson thanked Daniel and Mary. Through the kitchen window Daniel watched him drive away.

"Time for a proper cup of tea," Mary said, unhooking bigger, everyday cups from the dresser.

"Ralph," said his father, "get changed. We've got work to do."

Father and son resumed their usual labours. They said little. Later, having washed and changed into clean clothes, they took their places at the large table, where Mary dished up supper. Daniel said grace. They ate with appetite. The only conversation was between husband and wife and was confined to reports about farm routine. Ralph, silent, felt a notable tension. He longed to discuss Mr Richardson's visit, but he did not want to admit openly that he had been eavesdropping. The meal over and the table cleared, Daniel opened the large Bible and read out loud before a final prayer.

Ralph helped his mother by drying the dishes before he was free at last to go to his room. He was too busy with his thoughts to concentrate. He left his bedroom door open and strained to hear what his parents were talking about. He had not done this since he was much younger, but Mr Richardson's visit and the picture he had sketched of an exciting future had left Ralph in a disturbed state.

"Daniel," his mother said, "we need to talk about Mr Richardson's visit."

"There's nothing to discuss," said he husband. "Ralph's future is here, on the farm."

Ralph tiptoed as far as the top of the stairs. It was dark here. The light from his oil lamp had been turned to a glimmer, while the bigger lamp that hung from the kitchen ceiling threw its warm, yellow light downwards. It was chilly here on the landing, but Ralph hugged himself to keep warm.

"You heard what Mr Richardson said," Mary insisted. "Gifted, that's what he thinks of our son. Don't you think we owe him this chance?"

"Ralph's place is on this farm I've said it before, ever since he won that damned scholarship, that school has put poor ideas in his head!"

"Daniel!" Mary was shocked by the language. Ralph had never known him swear.

"I'm sorry," Daniel apologised. "You know how you always seem to fight me on this subject."

"And you are always pig-headed and blind to your son's best interest."

"How can you say that? I have worked all my life to hand this farm on to him. You and that –

that – school go on putting silly ideas in his head."

There was a silence after this. Ralph could imagine the two of them. His father, sitting in his usual old chair on one side of the range, would be smoking the one pipe he allowed himself before bedtime. His mother, her expression fixe, hopeless but obstinate.

"All right," said Daniel. "I know how much this means to you. We'll let him go ahead with his exams. He can even go ahead to prove the teachers are right. Let him prove he's one of the one in a hundred people."

Ralph's heart jumped with surprise, but his father had not finished.

"But that's where all this nonsense stops," his father declared. "When he leaves school with all those useless bits of paper, he comes to work full-time on the farm."

It was a partial victory. Ralph made his way back to his room. He was still too full of conflicting thoughts, hopes, feelings. He moved his lamp to the bedside cupboard, wrapped himself in the eiderdown and lay down. He began to formulate a plan. It would depend on doing especially well at school over the next year. He did not as yet know what would be involved in trying to get into university. He would only be able to do that if he could get some kind of grant or scholarship. His parents could not afford it. University or not, he would have to confront his father and tell him he would not work on the farm It would be difficult, a confrontation on a scale he feared, and his mother, her loyalties divided, would be badly hurt.

He turned down the wick of his lamp and blew it out. He lay awake, now warm, still unable to sleep. He heard his parents make their way to bed at the other end of the landing. Their argument was over and they were probably as tired as he was. The timbers creaked. Outside he could hear a pair of barn owls and occasional sounds from the cowshed. Some way off, a fox barked, a curiously lonely sound. It caused dogs to reply. At last, there was silence and he fell asleep.

Although he would never admit it even to himself, he was afraid of his father. Daniel had such firmly fixed ideas that he was unable to compromise. There had been one earlier occasion when Ralph had stood up to him and disagreed. He was fifteen at the time. The family had attended Chapel as usual on Sunday. The Sabbath was always a day of rest to be kept holy, Daniel said. Work on the farm was restricted to caring for the livestock, feeding, watering, milking, cleaning out, jobs which began at daybreak and were finished by about 9:30. Then came a late breakfast and, wearing their Sunday best clothes, all three squeezed into the front of the old pickup truck and drove to the service. It was the one time in the week when Ralph's parents took time to chat to their neighbours. Dorothy and Arthur Clarke's farm was about two miles from the Cobdens'.

"My word!" Dorothy observed. "Ralph is getting a big lad! Is he staying on at the grammar school?"

"He's due to take the school certificate next year," Mary said.

"How do you get to school?" Dorothy spoke directly to Ralph.

"On the school bus," he said. "It stops at the end of our lane."

"I'd have thought you would cycle. It's not that far, is it?"

"He doesn't have a bike," Mary said quickly answering for him.

"Our Colin was a keen cyclist," said Dorothy.

Colin, her son, was much older than Ralph, old enough to have enlisted in the RAF in 1942. The airfield where he was based had been bombed soon afterwards. Colin was killed. Arthur and Dorothy Clarke had been devastated. Friends and fellow worshippers had done their best to support and console them, pointing out they should be proud that their son had died doing his duty, helping to protect his precious England.

"His bike is still in the barn where he left it," Dorothy continued. "Neither of us thought about it. Would you like it, Ralph?"

"Are you sure?" Mary asked.

"Better it should be used. In fact," Dorothy said, "if Ralph comes home with us now, he can collect it and bring it back. What do you think?"

She walked over to where the two men were still talking about the need for rain. Her husband was surprised. He had not thought about the bike since his son's death more than seven years ago, but he agreed it made sense that it should be used. Soon, Ralph was sitting in the back seat of their comfortable family car on the way to the Clarke farm.

Arthur led the way to the back of the barn. The bicycle was leaning against the back wall where it had been for the past seven years. He brushed scraps of straw and dust from the saddle, the crossbar, and the handlebars, then he picked the machine up and shook off as much of the rest as he could.

"Probably needs a bit of oil," he said, "and I don't know what the tyres are like. I hope they haven't perished".

The tyres were in remarkably good condition. The bike, after all, had been stored in the dry and had been well looked after in the past. They seemed just a little soft, and the farmer used the bicycle pump to put more air in them before wheeling the bike out into the farmyard.

"This is very kind of you," Ralph said.

"It makes sense that it should be used. Not much point in letting it rot in the old barn So there you are, Ralph. I hope you like the dropped handlebars."

"They look very smart," Ralph said.

"What about the saddle? Is it the right height?"

Ralph did not know one way or the other.

"Best way to find out," said Arthur, "is to cock your leg over it. Have a go!"

Ralph hesitated. "I don't know how to ride a bike," he admitted.

"Haven't you ever learnt?" Arthur was astonished.

"I'll push it home and teach myself."

Arthur, still surprised, was looking at him. The Clarkes and the Cobdens were members of a small community. Arthur did not know this young boy very well, but he had heard about his progress at school, how he had won the scholarship to get there, how his parents had forked out the money for the school uniform, for the games kit, how they were clearly proud of the progress he was making. Next year he would be taking his School Certificate before he joined his father on the farm. According to Daniel, Ralph was also able to drive the family pickup round the farm, yet he couldn't ride a bike!

"Dinner won't be ready for an hour yet," Arthur said. "Get on and I'll hold the saddle while you try riding it across the yard."

Ralph did as he was told and Arthur, remembering the day many years before when he had taught his small son to ride on his first bike wanted more than anything to see Ralph take those first few wobbly yards on two wheels. Ralph, determined but uncertain, lost his balance several times, grazed one hand on the concrete. Dorothy, wondering where her husband had got to, emerged from the kitchen in her apron and watched, hands on hips, also remembering. She dried her eyes on her apron before pulling herself together and shouting encouragement. After half an hour, Arthur, puffing from running backwards and forwards, took his hand off the saddle and Ralph continued, unaware he was unsupported, until he reached the farm gate. He tried to brake, but only partly succeeded and was stopped when the front will hit the woodwork. He fell sideways but was unhurt.

"Well done!" Arthur said.

Dorothy was applauding.

"You were on your own," Arthur explained. "You're a quick learner. Now you need to practice a lot. Sorry, you will need to push it home as you planned, but you will soon be able to ride it anywhere. Well done lad!"

Ralph, rubbing his bruised hip with his scratched hand, thanked Arthur and Dorothy again and left them to enjoy their Sunday dinner. He pushed the bike as he started the two mile walk home. He was too excited to worry about the bruises or about the tear in one sock. He looked back as he reached the first bend. Dorothy and Arthur Clarke were still standing at their doorway, watching him. He could not see the way in which they were holding one another tightly, nor could he possibly know how the impromptu riding lesson had re-awoken the deep and inconsolable grief for both of them.

Within a week Ralph was riding his new bike quite competently. Unfortunately, the demands of schoolwork and helping on the farm left him very little time to take full advantage. He was expected to put in a full day's work every Saturday. He was also given homework to complete each weekend. In conversation with some of his fellow pupils, for the first time he began to regret and then resent the demands imposed upon him by his father. He was also beginning to have questions about religion, questions he dared not raise with his father. He saw contradictions in some of the teaching. Sometimes, listening to one of the preachers on a Sunday morning, he could not agree with the statements being made.

So, he screwed up his courage one afternoon, and suggested to his father that he might skip chapel the following Sunday morning.

"Miss chapel? What for? You can't do that. We always go to the morning service."

"A friend at school," Ralph lied," has asked me to go on a long bike ride with him up to the

Downs. It will take all day. The idea is to take a picnic."

"Who is this friend of yours?"

"Just one of the boys. His name is William."

"I don't really like the sound of this. I think you should come to chapel as usual."

"It might do me more good than one of those boring sermons."

"You'd do well to listen to what you are being told. I'm not sure I like the sound of this. It's that school of yours, putting silly thoughts in your head."

"Well, it's teaching me to think for myself."

" I can see that. That's exactly what I mean."

"Does that mean I can't go?"

Daniel picked up the bale of straw and thrust it at his son, forcing him to grab it and stagger. At another time it would have been a clumsy attempt at humour, but Ralph knew there was a degree of malice behind the gesture. No more was said and the two of them worked on until it was time for supper. That evening, in his room, Ralph heard his parents arguing. His mother, as he had hoped, persuaded his father to give way. She succeeded.

 It had taken unusual courage to speak as he had, though he was becoming more and more conscious that his fear of his father was not rational. Physically, he was bigger and stronger. Intellectually and educationally, he knew more. His father's knowledge and skills were restricted to farm work, but Ralph was beginning privately to challenge those, too. The Cobden farm was too small and old-fashioned. It needed serious investment, but Daniel would never borrow the large sums needed to bring it up to date. The future was in bigger units, anyway, larger herds, modern methods. Even the farmhouse still had no electricity. Ralph knew he would only provoke an argument or at best an outpouring of scorn from the older man, should he dare to comment on such matters. So, he wanted to escape.

For the first time that Sunday Ralph loaded his bike with a waterproof coat and a parcel of sandwiches and a flask of tea. On his bike he set off for the day, half an hour before his parents left for chapel. The roads were very quiet. He was already five miles from home by the time the church bells began to call worshippers to prayer. The solitude and freedom were exhilarating. He rode through a small village. A few of the villagers were on their way to church or walking their dogs and he saw the village shop was open for people to buy newspapers and cigarettes.

Shortly after this the road began the steep climb up the Downs. He was obliged to push his bike. He was in no hurry and stopped from time to time to look back. At last, he reached a less steep slope. He remounted and continued until he was on a flatter part of the road. On either side there were grassy banks, surmounted by thickets of hazel. A quarter of a mile later a chalky lane led to the left. To either side of the lane there were fields, apparently uncultivated. It was quite difficult to ride because the surface was deeply rutted on either side and Ralph found it simpler to walk once more. Past the fields the lane became a much simpler and less rutted track which led ever upwards towards the smooth, grassy summit. The path ran parallel to the true summit, on the southern side. He pushed his bike over the turf until he reached the very top. He lay the bike carefully on its side and sat down to admire the view. It was like looking at a map. He gazed in wonder for a long time. He traced the journey he had made back from the foot of the hill through the village and beyond. The houses looked like small, wooden blocks, not like buildings in which people lived. The air was clear, and he could see for miles. There, snaking its way through the patchwork fields, he could see the road all the way back to his home. He identified the fields. At this distance he could not distinguish individual animals, but he could see them against the dull green of the meadow. It was the sheer scale of this scene which held his attention. To his left he could see the outskirts of the town which he knew must be at least eight miles away It was a bit like an unsightly, black mark, out of place in all these multicoloured fields, so neatly bordered by hedges. Individual trees were scattered throughout the Weald. Even further away than the town, he could see the same colours as they receded into the distance. The brightness faded the further away he looked until, in the very far distance, he could see another range of hills, the North Downs. Distance made them look hazy and blue.

Transfixed, Ralph sat and gazed for a long time before turning his attention to the hill on which he sat. There was no sound coming from the valley. The church bells had long since fallen silent and he pictured to himself the scene inside the chapel. His parents would be leaning forward in their pine pews, like the rest of the congregation, all listening intently to the prayer, only their backs visible. It would be solemn, and Ralph allowed himself to use the word boring. At the thought he threw his arms wide and shouted in exaltation at the sense of freedom he felt. He fell on his back and gazed at the cloudless sky. The turf on which he lay was resilient and springy. It smelled of thyme, clean and refreshing. Birds flitted across his vision. He could not distinguish their songs. From the valley below the harsh cawing of a rookery was easily identifiable. But, lying here on this soft but slightly prickly turf, he could hear the rustling and chirruping of insects, grasshoppers landed on his hands, flying insects buzzed. Ralph had never experienced such peace.

After a very long time he sat up and unpacked the sandwiches he had brought with him. He had never been so happy. He did not want to move; however, he stood up at last, brushed himself down, and brushed at the bits of grass and myriad insects that seemed to have collected on his trousers, then he retrieved his bicycle and walked with it a short distance further along the path. It forked, continuing along the crest of the hill, or diving steeply down on the southern side into a wood. Ralph headed downwards, although it meant a steep climb later. To his surprise the wood consisted of large, ancient, yew trees. Only on the outskirts were the yews interspersed here and there with glossy holly. The foliage in the wood was so dense that little light penetrated and the ground beneath the boughs was carpeted with dead needles and twigs, brown, they crunched beneath his feet. The contrast with the sunny hillside was startling. Ralph sensed these trees were truly ancient and they filled him with awe. He felt strangely uneasy. Some of the branches, almost too heavy to support themselves, grew outwards from near the base of the huge trunk for many feet at no more than head height. He walked as far as the gnarled and twisted trunk to look for a while The bark, flaking in places, was amazingly varied, brown, red, green. But it was the silence that unnerved him. He turned and headed back into the sunlight.

He pushed his precious bike back up to where the path forked and sat until he began to feel both hungry and thirsty. He had no more food left and he had not thought to save at least one sandwich, nor a mouthful of tea. There was nothing for it but to go home. He was reluctant to go. He would come back. He would also go to the library to find the name of the wood. He did not know how important this experience was to prove, though it left him with an unforgettable memory. He negotiated the path between the fields and regained the smoother road. Now he could pedal more quickly, and he felt the wind in his face. He reached the steep hill up which he had pushed his bike and was a little frightened at the prospect of the descent, but he gripped the handlebars with his fingers on the brake levers and began. Soon the speed became intoxicating and he found himself shouting with joy as he sped down the hill. He rode through the village. One or two people watched him ride past. He glimpsed a cricket match but it was screened by hedges. Then the countryside became more familiar – fields with cattle grazing, all lying dreamily and chewing the cud. Finally, hot, and tired, he reached the farm. As he opened the farm gate and wheeled his bicycle through, he felt a mixture of relief and regret.

"The evening milking is in half an hour," his father announced. "You need to change."

"Give the boy a chance to get in," his mother said. "You look hot! I'll get you a glass of lemonade. Are you hungry? Have you eaten everything? I'll get you a piece of cake."

Ralph ate hungrily.

"Where did you get to with your friend?" Mary asked. "Did you get to the Downs?"

"Yes," Ralph said. He had forgotten his imaginary friend, William. "It was quite hard work climbing the hill to the top."

"Well, you've worked up an appetite."

Ralph drank a second glass of lemonade, put the plate back on the table and went upstairs to change into his working clothes. He joined his father in the milking parlour. They were still milking by hand, though Daniel had been thinking of installing a milking machine. Ralph, his head leaning against the cow's flank, was still thinking of the view from the top of the Downs. Tomorrow he would be back at school. He enjoyed school. He liked the teachers and the work. He got on reasonably well with his fellow pupils, although he had no close friends. Many of them came from wealthier homes, had parents with jobs he knew little about – solicitors, doctors, even teachers. They sometimes were driven to school in cars which contrasted with his own parents' truck. They talked about parties or football or television, none of which was part of Ralph's world. He felt at a disadvantage. He knew he was doing well at his schoolwork, but he suspected that the teachers were being deliberately kind, knowing about his background.

He did not dare suggest skipping chapel the next week, though he longed to escape and enjoy the same freedom. When he raised the subject three weeks later, his father objected, as Ralph expected, and his mother once more had argued his case. It distressed him that he should be the cause of the arguments between his parents. They never seemed to argue about anything else.

The biggest argument came when, at the age of 16, he took his mock school certificates. He did exceptionally well. His parents, invited to a parents' evening went to the school, uncomfortable in their Sunday best. Daniel had to be persuaded to attend. "What's the point?" he asked. "We know he has done well. That means he will do okay when he takes the real exam. But then he will be sixteen, time for him to leave school and join us on the farm properly."

His wife and his teachers had other plans.

"I hope," said the Headmaster, "you will agree to Ralph's joining the Sixth Form. If these results are anything to go by, he has a promising future. He will do extremely well, I'm sure. He is especially good at English. He writes really interesting essays already. He has a real understanding and appreciation of poetry as well as other literature."

"Really?" Mary was delighted and proud to hear this, but Daniel had other things on his mind.

"Poetry won't help him run a farm," he said. "No, it's bad enough having to wait until he's sixteen to join me. Ralph's place is on the farm and that's where he will be next year, no poetry. You've done a good job, I give you that. And I suppose he will be able to help with the bookkeeping and all that sort of thing."

"Oh, I hope you'll change your mind," said Mr Richardson. "Ralph is a really promising pupil. I hope you won't stand in his way."

"He's needing on the farm." Daniel was adamant.

This was no surprise to Ralph, though he longed to stay on at school. That evening, after he had gone to his room, he heard his mother and father for the first time raise their voices in a furious argument.

"Daniel Cobden!" his mother shouted, "you are a hypocrite! You were in chapel on Sunday, weren't you?"

"What are you talking about, woman?" his father said. "What do you mean? Of course, I was in chapel."

"And you heard the preacher?"

"Mr Marlow? Yes, I heard him. I always listen to the sermon, you know that."

"And what was it about?"

"One of the parables." Daniel was trying to remember.

"The parable of the talents," his wife reminded him.

"What are you trying to say?"

"Your own son, Ralph, has been given a precious talent by God," Mary exclaimed, "and you won't let him develop it. If he's got this ability, surely it must be God's wish for him to use it to the full."

There was a lull in the argument. Ralph, listening attentively, waited.

"I never thought of it that way," Daniel admitted.

"It seems to me, Daniel, you don't think about anything much except the farm."

"It's our future and his".

" What if it isn't really his future at all? What if God has something else in store

"I wish you wouldn't keep bringing God into this."

"What is more important, your farm or your son's happiness?"

"Are you saying Ralph won't be happy as a farmer?"

"Who knows? Have you asked him?"

"He's only a boy! He doesn't know his own mind yet."

"I think if you asked him, he'll say he wants to stay on in the sixth form. I think that's true at least."

"You've always had a soft spot where he is concerned. What about his duty?"

"You can't accuse him of not pulling his weight. He works all the hours he can as well as having to keep up with all the schoolwork. You even resent giving him pocket money, and his only time off is Sunday."

"I never had pocket money as a boy."

"Daniel, things have changed! The world is changing. Even you must admit that. Nothing stays the same. I'm just saying our son deserves the chance."

"I'll think about it."

He hated it when his parents quarrelled. It was a rare occurrence and seemed almost always to be triggered by him and his future. Mary, as often happened, got her way. Ralph continued into the sixth form. It was at the end of the first term that Mr Richardson had phoned to discuss the possibility of working towards a further step on the educational ladder.

"We are quite concerned about Ralph," he said, setting Mary's heart fluttering with anxiety. "He seems exhausted. He actually fell asleep in class the other day. Is he getting enough sleep?"

Mary explained how Ralph came home every afternoon and then worked with his father until supper time.

"I see," said Mr Richardson. "Well, that explains a lot. He has always avoided taking part in any out-of-school activities. We thought he was just not especially sociable."

"He has to get home."

"Is there no way he can do his school work when he gets home?"

"The farm work has to be done in daylight."

"I understand that, Mrs Cobden, but I'll be frank with you. Ralph's work in the sixth form is designed to stretch him. He is probably one of the brightest and most promising boys we have had here, but he will not be able to cope as things are."

"Oh!"

"It is early yet, but I would hope your son could do exceptionally well. University is a real possibility, but not unless he can have more time to work on his courses."

Daniel was obdurate. Ralph's future lay in the farm. What was this posh schoolmaster thinking of, interfering? Mary did her very best to persuade him. She pointed out that Ralph would be eighteen the following year and would sit his Senior Certificate by then. Could they not employ an extra hand for that time? She mentioned a sixty-year- old farmhand, a cowman they both knew, who had recently lost his job when his employer sold their farm.

Daniel refused to consider it at first. This time the argument became a noisy and frightening row. Mary made serious threats. At last Daniel gave way, but Ralph was aware of a change at home. His father was not a great conversationalist at the best of times, but now he and his wife seemed to speak only when it was essential.

However, Ralph was now free to give his schoolwork more attention. He thanked his mother for the tea she gave him when he got home, then took it to his bedroom until he was called to supper. It was a dreary meal, heavy with resentment. As soon as the Bible reading and prayers were over, he went back to his room. He had a great deal of reading to do, but he enjoyed it, escaping into worlds and situations that caused him to forget his surroundings. He loved poetry, the use of words that sharpened his vision.

His teachers were delighted. Ralph seemed to eat the work with a rare enthusiasm. The next step in his progress came when he was told he was to spend three days in Oxford to sit an Entrance Exam. For a term his teachers prepared him, explaining and practising the kind of papers he would be faced with.

Daniel refused outright to pay for Ralph to go. Mary was in tears, but Daniel was adamant. The boy would be leaving school in a matter of months, it would be ridiculous to fill his head with such fantasies. But Mr Richardson told Mary on the telephone that the school had a special fund which could be used for such occasions. Daniel was furious but had been outplayed.

Ralph had never travelled by train. The whole experience was novel, and he was nervously excited all the time. The written papers were taken in the vast, medieval Hall of Christ Church College. The candidates sat on benches and worked side by side in silence, a silence disturbed occasionally as a large log fell with a crash in the huge fireplace. Ralph completed four such papers and then faced an interview in the hall of his own college. When an usher called him in, he walked nervously to the far end. Behind a very long refectory table nine men faced him. They all wore long gowns, some with bright colours and fur round the collar.

"Please sit down, Mr Cobden." The man in the middle spoke. Ralph sat on the solitary chair.

"Cobden is a great name," the man continued. "Let me just introduce my colleagues here, then perhaps you can tell us a little more about your predecessor."

This was not what Ralph had expected or prepared for, but he had looked into Richard Cobden. He explained that a succession of bad harvests, the Napoleonic Wars, and the imposition of high prices by landowners and middlemen, had pushed prices high. Bread was a staple food, but flour was expensive. Richard Cobden set up an organisation to persuade the government to repeal the existing Corn Laws. To help bring about change he established The Economist. But it was probably also the effect of the Irish Potato Famine that pushed the Prime Minister, Robert Peel, to act in 1846.

At this point Ralph stopped, realising that he had been talking like someone giving a lecture. But the row of black-gowned figures was watching and listening.

The questions that followed were more closely concerned with the set books and with his wider reading. When, after twenty minutes, he was thanked, he walked the length of the hall, his shoes noisy on the flagged floor, and escaped into the fresh air. He was trembling.

On the train home he looked out on the fields and woods, and he was now sure he did not want to spend his life farming. The brief glimpse of academic life was what he earnestly wished for. It was, he knew, only a brief taste, but the undergraduate's room he had lived in for three days was full of books, the quad outside the window was like a medieval cloister, no cows lowing, no cockerels crowing. Instead, there had been a few, wonderful minutes when he has spoken to eminent lecturers and even professors and they had listened with interest and engaged in conversation almost as though he was an equal. He had been treated with respect and called Mr Cobden. The Porter and the Scout on his staircase called him "Sir." Whatever the cost in terms of a fight with his father, his mind was made up. He would not work on the farm next year or in the future.

Matters worsened soon after he returned home. Ralph was once more summoned to the Headmaster's study. When he walked in, the Headmaster and two of his best-liked teachers, Mr Williams, who taught English and Mr Jenkins, who taught History, stood and welcomed him.

"Congratulations!" Mr Richardson held out a hand.

Ralph was not clear what he had done to deserve this. Mr Richardson waved a piece of paper. "Of course," he said, "you won't know until you get home and pick up your post. You've done it, Ralph! You've been offered a place at Queen's!"

The next few minutes passed in a blur. Mr Williams, who had encouraged Ralph's interest in poetry and his reading, was smiling broadly. The letter referred specifically to the positive impression he had made when he talked about Richard Cobden, the information which Mr

Jenkins had helped him find. Ralph staggered out of the study in a daze. He did not return to the classroom. Instead, he wandered to a partially secluded area of the school grounds and sat with his back to a tree, trying to think about this astounding news.

The offer was conditional on his achieving the highest grades in the coming exams. His "mock" results had been good, but he could not be completely sure he would do as well in the real exams. He would do his best. He knew he would not only have to fight his father, if he wanted to take up this place, he would never be forgiven. His mother would be affected. She would be proud of him and plead his case, but his father had made his views crystal clear. He would never give way. And that led to the biggest obstacle of all – money. Ralph had no idea what it would cost to spend three years at the University. He only knew his father would not provide the money. Mr Richardson had spoken of scholarships. He needed to know more. The offer was also to be deferred for two years, allowing time to do his National Service. His father said he would be exempt from National Service as an agricultural worker when he joined him on the farm. As things stood that would be next year! The very thought was bitter. Ralph, on his own in the deserted grounds, drew up his knees and hugged them. A plan began to form. It was desperate, but it might work. Next year would require all his courage and could well mark a complete break with his father. Ralph felt a momentary flash of pity for Daniel, whose hard work and dedication to the farm merited respect, but this was too important to be affected by such feelings. At stake was his future happiness. He stood up, brushed the grass from his trousers, and went back to the classroom.

Ralph's teachers were slightly baffled by the change in his behaviour over his last year at the school. He worked with a determination they had not seen before, but he did not appear to enjoy it as much. When he sat at the small table in the school hall and wrote answers to the questions presented, it was with the same ability as in the past. He appeared not to enjoy it, however and would say nothing when asked what he thought of the questions or of his answers. In July he reached his eighteenth birthday. On the day that he received his higher certificate results he also received a large, brown envelope marked OHMS. Inside was a formal letter requiring him to report for a full, medical examination in the nearby town. He was to serve his National Service a short time later.

"Is there a phone number?" asked his father. "I expect they'll want me to certify that you really are an agricultural worker."

"But I'm not," said Ralph.

His father stared at him, uncomprehending. "What are you talking about, boy? The agreement was that you would work for me when you left school. Well, you have left school. You won't want to do National Service, and we agreed that you won't go ahead with all that university nonsense."

"I never agreed," Ralph said.

His father stared at him. "We had all this out a year ago," he insisted. "I need you on the farm and that's that. I've supported you long enough. If you don't tell these people, I shall."

"You can tell them that I work for you on the farm?"

Daniel nodded. "Yes," he said. "As from Monday. You know what's to be done, and it won't do you any harm to put in a full day's work for once."

"No."

"No? What are you saying? You don't want a holiday before you start, surely? You've had it easy for the last two years. You can start on Monday."

"I'm not an agricultural worker." Ralph, his face stiff with determination and fear of the most serious confrontation of his life, was determined.

"Look here, boy," his father, still more surprised than angry as yet, was not going to give in easily. "Maybe I've been too easy on you. All this fancy learning you've been doing at that school has probably put some silly ideas in your head. Time you came down to earth, Ralph. We have a farm to run. Use those precious brains of yours to turn it into a better farm for all of us. Time to forget all those fanciful ideas."

"I'm not doing it, dad."

Daniel was beginning to lose patience. "You don't have a choice," he said. "You're an agricultural worker on this farm. If you don't tell them that, I will. That exempts you for doing this stupid, National Service. Do you really want to spend two years learning how to march up and down?"

"But you don't employ me!"

"What do you mean? Until this last year you were putting your fair share every day. It was only because your mother intervened that I let you off. You know almost as much about farming as – well, as a lot of other workers I know."

"You've never paid me properly," Ralph said, his face still stiff as he continued to fight his corner. "I bet you've never shown me as an employee on any official forms, never paid a national Insurance contribution for me, certainly never paid me a regular wage or PAYE."

Daniel began to look flustered. "Those are technicalities," he said. "I'll have to do all those things now. Don't try to be clever with me."

"Too late, dad," Ralph said firmly. "You've got no documentary evidence to show that I am already a farm worker. You've used me as a help, but you've never paid me a regular wage."

"I've given you a home and looked after you all your life!" Daniel was almost indignant. Ralph was thinking, my God! He really believes what he's saying. He thinks, because he's my father, I am obliged to do whatever he wants, work for nothing.

"You can argue all you like," Daniel said. "You start work on Monday morning. Give me that form. I'll write and put them straight."

But Ralph had already tucked the letter into his pocket, and he turned his back and walked away.

This encounter had taken place in the farm kitchen and Mary had witnessed it but said nothing. When Ralph disappeared up to his room, Daniel left by the outside door, slamming it behind him. Mary slumped into a seat. She had been expecting something of this sort. She was once more torn in two. She understood and sympathised with Ralph's ambitions. Far more than her husband, she understood just how much Ralph had achieved already. He could do so much better for himself, and she had to admit, he was now a man, old enough to make his own decisions. The next five years were mapped out for him – two years' military training which, she supposed, must have some value. She hoped that the Cold War would not heat up, but nobody was quite sure about that. Ralph would then have three years at university, three years which were unique. He was, she often remembered, one in a hundred, a very clever young man, someone she loved and was immensely proud of. But Ralph's future happiness could only come, it seemed, at the cost of the enormous disappointment to Daniel. With all his limitations, Daniel was a good man at heart. She had known and loved him for more than thirty years, since they were both teenagers. It pained her to see him hurt so badly. She heaved a great sigh and made herself a pot of tea. Ultimately, she would support Ralph in his decision. It would cause a terrible break in relationships. Daniel would never forgive Ralph and it might even break him to face the end of the Cobden farm. She cried a little. Then she pulled herself together and made a start on the evening meal.

The following morning Ralph helped his father as usual. They worked in silence until breakfast. As Daniel drank a last mug of tea, he stated, "I'll need a hand fixing the gate. The hinges are shot."

"You'll have to give Harry Waters a call then," said Ralph. "As soon as I've changed, I'm off."

His parents were both startled.

"I thought..." his father began.

"Just because I helped with the milking, you shouldn't get the wrong idea."

The two men glared at one another. Then Ralph pushed his chair back and walked to the door.

"Off where?" shouted his father. Surprise gave way rapidly to anger.

"Ralph ignored him as he continued to shout after him. Mary, unable to bear it, clapped her hands to her ears, crying protests, begging her husband to stop. This open fight was destroying her. When Ralph failed to respond,

Daniel struck the wall with a clenched fist with such force that the wallpaper tore and he left a dent in the plaster. Mary had never seen such rage and was afraid, but Daniels swore, shocking her further, before striding angrily out to the yard.

Ralph reappeared half an hour later. He had two small parcels which he had tied with string – clothes. So, he meant it!

Before Mary could say anything, he spoke.

"Mum," he said, "have you got any money? I don't need much, maybe a pound. Sorry to ask, but he's such a Scrooge. I've had nothing from him in weeks".

Mary fumbled in her purse and handed three one- pound notes to her son. "It's all I've got left of the housekeeping," she said. "Where are you going?"

"I think I know where I can get a job for a few months," Ralph explained. "It's a market garden the other side of Porton. The manager has a son I know at school."

"But where will you stay?"

"There's accommodation, too. Don't worry. I'll ring you when I get there."

"When will I see you?"

"You can catch a bus into Porton and I'll buy you a meal with my first pay packet."

He hugged her and left, packing his belongings in the pannier bags of his bike. Mary stood at the farm gate and watched him ride away. She dried her eyes at last and turned back to the kitchen door. Daniel, who had seen Ralph leave from where he was working in the dairy, approached his wife. This time it was Marry who lost her temper.

"Look what you've done, you stupid man!" She tried to shout, but the words were strangled, and the tears returned, this time accompanied by deep, reaching sobs and she made her way blindly indoors to the parlour. There she collapsed on the chaise longue. Daniel was at a loss. He followed only as far as the kitchen, where he sat, not knowing what to do.

Ralph never returned to Cobden Farm all the time his father was alive. As planned, he met his mother, who brought him more of his belongings, but there not many. Daniel refused to speak to his son, though he continued to nurse the hope that one day Ralph would see the error of his ways. He was the Prodigal Son. When he returned, as Daniel was sure he would, it would be to resume his destined career and enjoy his heritage. He was to keep this private belief until the day he died.

Mary, a Christian believer, had taken her marriage vows before God. The love and respect she had felt for her stubborn husband had been severely battered by the fight with Ralph. She loved her son and wanted his happiness more than anything, but it had come at a dreadful cost. She could not forgive Daniel. His implacable rejection of Ralph's desires changed their relationship. She became impatient, un co-operative. She did the usual chores, fed the chickens, helped dig the garden, but she stopped singing as she worked. She began to look older. Her hair, once brown, turned grey.

Ralph saw the changes and felt some guilt but ascribed it mainly to his father's stubbornness.

He spent three months on the market garden and enjoyed it. It was wonderful to take the small, brown envelope every Friday and pour out the money. Most of it he saved for his university fund.

At last, he was required to join the Army. He left his bike at the market garden and travelled to Aldershot.

Part Two

The Land Rover came to a halt. Chris, staring over the bonnet at the pile of bricks and flints, which had once been walls, was speechless. Ralph, at the wheel, waited. He was not expecting a positive reaction, nor did he get one.

"Normally," Chris said at last, "I would be asking you if this was some kind of practical joke. But you don't have much sense of humour these days, unsurprisingly I suppose. But tell me, Ralph, you're not absolutely determined."

"Absolutely."

"But this is literally miles from anywhere. You won't be able to live in a ruin."

"I have the money. I can rebuild it. I know it won't be easy. It will just cost a lot. As for being miles from anywhere, that's the whole point. I've decided to call it "The Hermitage". That's what it's going to be, somewhere I can retreat."

Chris turned in his seat to look at his friend. The past five years had been more than many people could have withstood. The most serious blow had been when Gillian, Ralph's vivacious young wife, had developed a brain tumour which proved inoperable. They had had little more than three years together. Gillian had helped him recover from the trauma of his father's untimely death and the sale of the farm. His mother, having seen her husband die a particularly painful and unexpected death, had suffered first a stroke and then a fatal heart attack. Ralph had dealt with two funerals and the demanding process of selling the family farm. It had, Chris thought, knocked most of the stuffing out of him.

Chris had first met Ralph when they were doing National Service. They were both looking forward to taking up places at Oxford. The friendship blossomed and continued. Chris had been Best Man at the wedding. Daniel, Ralph's father, had not attended. Gillian had done her best to persuade him, but the farmer was stubborn. It was obvious that Ralph was immensely fond of his mother.

Chris, now a qualified pharmacist, worked in the pharmacy in the hospital. Ralph, having sold the farm, helped his mother settle into a small house in the town. She had her friends from the chapel nearby, but she was not very happy, living away from the farmhouse which had been her home for all her married life. Although Daniel had become morose and argumentative, she had been married to him for forty years. His death was one of those accidents that occur from time to time on a farm. His old bull, Caesar, in his small enclosure, was restless and Daniel looked over the fence and tried to soothe him by talking to him. The animal appeared to have something wrong with his left hind hoof. Caesar had never been difficult to handle, at least not for Daniel, so he entered the pen to take a closer look. He bent to examine the leg. Caesar swung his great head and Daniel had no chance of avoiding the horn which struck him in the side under his ribs. The bull then lifted his massive head, causing more damage before Daniel fell to the floor. Harry, the farmhand, had seen Daniel entered the pen and had shouted a warning which Daniel ignored. Now Harry risked injury himself. He opened the gate, grabbed the shoulders of Daniel's jacket, and pulled him to safety. He was shouting to Mary as he did so, but his effort was too late. Daniel died before the ambulance arrived.

"He could have had the bull polled," Ralph told Chris, "But he thought it was unnatural. He liked to see the horns."

Daniel's death had caused a serious crisis. Although Harry was happy to stay on and help, the day-to-day running of the farm was beyond Mary's capability. For the first time in many years Ralph had been obliged to return. He had served the first year of apprenticeship as a journalist on the local newspaper, a humble enough job, but one which he had chosen. It would lead, he expected, to more challenging assignments in due course. And, although the humdrum reports which he was required to provide were hardly great literature, he was still writing. That, and his new wife, kept him busy. He met his mother on a regular basis, but never at the farm. Now he could not avoid returning. Gillian remained in their flat. She was a nurse and there was little she could do on the farm. For several weeks they met only at weekends.

It was obvious to Ralph that his mother would be unable to cope with the farm. He told her the only sensible thing to do would be to sell up. To his surprise she took this decision without objection. She was concerned at the prospect of having to find somewhere else to live, but the proceeds of the farm, as he pointed out, would allow her to choose a comfortable place. He did not realise until he talked to the family solicitor, that his father had also invested in a large life insurance policy. Arthur Clarke agreed to buy the cattle, solving one of the major problems. Other livestock was much easier to dispose of. The property itself, including the farmhouse, was put up for auction. As Ralph was aware, the buyer would need to invest not only in the farmhouse, but also in the land, which needed improvement. However, there was a shortage of land for sale, and Mary was finally settled in a small house in town, not far from her son and daughter-in-law. She was, as she said, "comfortably off." Her death, two years later, was even more traumatic for Ralph. He was unable to forget that the antagonism between himself and his father had caused great pain to his mother. It had clearly caused a rift between husband and wife, as well as between father and son. He had thought to escape the consequences by running away, but he had left his mother to live in a never-resolved relationship. He, Ralph, was also left with regret and guilt because he had never been reconciled with his father.

At least he had Gillian. So, when her frequent migraines caused the consultant to express serious concern, and she was diagnosed too late with a brain tumour, Ralph's world collapsed around him. Chris, who loved them both, did his best to listen and to talk. Ralph was suicidal for a while, unable to see anything worth living for. Mary, like her husband, had been well insured, and Ralph found himself quite wealthy. Her house was now sold. The proceeds from the farm sale and now three life insurances meant that at least he did not need to worry about his financial future. For several months he was deeply depressed, however. His only distraction lay in reading. He had many books, including poetry, poetry which concerned nature. His long-standing love of the Downs was reflected in his reading. Numerous writers were connections with this part of the country, from Rudyard Kipling to the Bloomsbury Group.

He never went back to his work as a journalist.

Now he seemed to Chris to be reawakening from this nightmare of depression. Their friendship was deep and lasting. When Ralph told him that he had made some decisions, Chris listened.

"I want to be closer to the Downs," Ralph said. "I asked three estate agents to keep a look out for a suitable property. One of them has found a possible site. I have also bought a second-hand Land Rover. It's more suitable for the place in question."

"Right," Chris said. "Where is it?"

"It's an old cottage. Well, it's pretty well derelict, but planning permission will be easier, because there is or has been a building there already."

"Derelict? What about things like electricity?"

"No, and it would be too expensive to be connected to the grid. I shall probably have to install a generator."

"It sounds like a full-scale rebuilding project, and horribly expensive!"

"It probably will be," said Ralph, "but what's money for?"

Chris had no answer. His only concern was that this cottage, once built or rebuilt, might be too remote. He did not voice his objections until he had seen the place. The rough, bumpy track seemed to go on for ever and, when Ralph pointed out the ruin he proposed to buy, Chris was simply aghast. Recognising the unsteady state of Ralph's mind, Chris was uncertain what to say.

"Have you thought this through?" he asked at last. "I know you want to get away from people at the moment, but will things change? Don't you think you may regret it after a while? And to be honest, I can't see anyone wanting to buy it, even after you have done it up. If you decide you need to return to town or somewhere a little closer to other people, you may well find yourself stuck with a white elephant."

"You, of all people surely understand. I feel as if the world has tried to kick me to death. It very nearly succeeded. In fact, you have been one of the principal people who have talked me out of killing myself. That doesn't mean that I want to take on the world again, not now or at any time in the future. These ancient hills have a history of their own. The Celts who lived here three thousand years ago cut down all the trees. You'd have thought that would be anathema to me. I love trees, but then three thousand years of grazing by sheep has produced something really special, beautiful and peaceful. It's where I want to be. It will cost a bit, and it will take time, but this is where I belong."

It would be pointless, Chris thought, to argue.

"So, what do you plan to do while the builders get to work?"

"Just over there," said Ralph, pointing to the south, "there's an old quarry. It's close enough for me to keep an eye on the builders and far enough away so they won't disturb me too badly. I'm getting an old caravan brought up here. Come and have a look."

They left the vehicle on the track and walked across the springy turf. The quarry had not been worked for decades. It was small, but big enough to accommodate a caravan, no doubt.

Grass and small saplings had invaded the flat space.

"Ralph," Chris exclaimed, "how are you going to get a caravan in here?"

"That's my first job," Ralph said. "You'd be surprised how quickly all this can be tamed. A few hours' work with the scythe and an axe, and Bob's your uncle."

For the first time in months Chris heard a new, positive tone. Perhaps this project had some merit after all. Perhaps it would give his friend a new sense of purpose, something which would make him work and plan for a future. It might prove an expensive mistake, but if it rescued Ralph from the dark despair which had already almost overcome him, he, Chris, would not dissuade him. They walked along the top of the quarry face. It was not very deep, just deep enough to conceal something like a caravan.

"What are you doing about water or sanitation?" he asked.

"I'll have to fetch the water from the nearest service station for the moment," Ralph said. "That won't be a problem. I'll need half a dozen jerry cans. The loo is more of a problem. I have to get one of those portable things. And then I'll have to find a suitable spot to dig a hole. Fortunately, this is down the slope from the cottage."

"What about the cottage itself? There won't be any drains there, and what about running water? I understand your plan to buy a generator, but it might be a bit noisy, if what you're looking for is peace and quiet. I suppose, if you had electricity, you could also have a deep freeze and collect food at intervals."

"See? It is feasible. You are beginning to think the same way as me."

Chris grinned. "I wouldn't go quite that far but I know you well enough not to argue," he said. "It's good to see you thinking positively about the future. I'm not the only one who has been worried about you, you know."

He regretted it as soon as he spoke. Ralph's expression changed as the reference to his recent experience was brought back.

"I know that," he said, his voice almost expressionless.

They made their way back to the Land Rover and Ralph drove down the jolting path to the road. It was virtually impossible to hold a conversation in the cab.

Journal

Well, I've done it. The past few weeks have been very busy. It was all necessary, but I can't say I enjoyed it, having to deal with so many people. For the past six weeks at least, I just yearned for this moment. Here I am, sitting at my typewriter, recording my thoughts and feelings. A couple of hundred yards away there is noise as the builders – or should I call them destroyers? – get on with clearing away the old rubble. Every so often a lorry comes jolting up the track to be loaded. It's hardly the kind of peace and quiet I want, but I console myself with the thought that it might be quieter once the construction begins. There is certainly plenty to do. Building a new cottage on the remains of the old is the least of the problems. It will be a simple place, small and built to my specifications: kitchen, bathroom, living room and study/library downstairs and two bedrooms upstairs. That much is simple. More complicated (and more noise!) when it comes to a borehole for water and site for the septic tank. It has all required lots of thinking and then getting the necessary planning permissions. They have even insisted the flints must be re-used as far as possible although the inside walls can be breezeblock. It's a good thing I have agents to complete all the negotiations. Graham Morton is the project manager. He has strict instructions never to disturb me unless there is a real emergency. I have managed to resist the advice of everyone, including Chris. to instal a telephone line "for emergencies" they say. It would completely defeat the object of the move. This is not yet the peace I was looking for. I can only hope it will be worth it in the end.

When the workmen have finished for the day and driven off down the track, I have a little foretaste of the future. The caravan is a little cramped, but perfectly adequate. Best of all, while there is still the light in the sky, I can at last enjoy the solitude and walk on my own on this wonderful turf. Sometimes I even venture out in the night. That's when the rabbits come out. They scuttle away at the sight of my torch which I use to avoid falling into any of the holes. From the top of the Down I can look into the valley and see the yellow light spilling out from the windows. To the west there is a glow from the streetlamps in the town. On a clear night the sky is still dark enough for me to look up at the stars. I relish walking back to the van in the silence. I am less happy when it comes to getting into bed. Despite my best efforts, I cannot shake off the memories. It's as though the roles of Heathcliff and Cathy have been reversed and I want to open the caravan door and shout her name into the darkness. I usually try to switch my attention to the building that is going on just a few yards away from me. Sometimes it works, but not usually for long.

Writing this journal is another attempt to shift my attention away from grief and melancholy. It has no other purpose and no one else will ever read it. I wasn't at all surprised when everybody argued against this move. Dr Thornton expressed what many people were thinking. He said, "You can't escape your memories by moving from one place to another. You will take them all with you. Only you will be isolated. There will be nobody to help you when you need it most. This is a bad idea. Please reconsider." He wasn't telling me anything I had not thought of myself. I'm not expecting to run away from my past. How could

I possibly want to forget Gillian, anyway? It's just that all the advice, however well meant, is like so much noise preventing me from thinking. I'm not stupid. I just want to get away from the noise both literally and metaphorically.

For the moment this little caravan is my home. It provides all the necessities. I quite like this quarry. It's small and not very deep, but the walls are just deep enough to shut out most of the noise from the builders during the day. It is also sheltered, or will be, if the weather turns unpleasant. I have already spent some time clearing the floor of the quarry itself. One of my aims is to grow a lot of my own food. I bought tools, but the bottom of the quarry is literally rock hard. I am having to rethink that plan. I shall get a load of topsoil delivered together with old railway sleepers to make the sides of my garden. I reckon I need about nine inches of soil. I'll need to keep it in good condition by having a load of manure delivered from time to time or, something I prefer, by making a fair - sized compost heap. It's just as well I learned how to garden on the farm as a boy.

The one thing I miss at the moment are my books. They are all packed up in boxes in storage, waiting for the cottage to be completed. I have only one or two, mostly reference books. I could order more, but that involves driving into town, something I don't intend to do more than essential. I shall have to grit my teeth to face the traffic. There are a few visits I must make to the solicitors and the bank. The Post Office won't deliver this far off the beaten track, and that means that I have to have a post office box in town. I shall have to empty that, I suppose. There are ways around most problems. One purpose of moving up here is to make it difficult for people to visit me. I just don't want them. Chris is a possible exception. But even Chris is not prepared to tackle the track, which is becoming steadily worse as the builders' lorries are obliged to use it. The old Land Rover lurches and staggers in four-wheel-drive. I may have to get the worst of the ruts filled in when they have finished. If Chris wants to visit, he will have to park his car at the beginning of the track and walk. It's between a quarter and half a mile, enough to put off casual visitors. I won't know when he's coming, of course, so it could be that I'm out. In that case, he'll just have to make himself at home and wait as long as he can. I'll drive him back to as far his car later. I am certainly not going to get a telephone line installed.

They estimate it will take about twelve months to get the cottage ready. We'll see. A lot will depend on the petty officials, the inspector who will come to check on building regulations, the people who will check that the water supply is drinkable – it certainly should be after being filtered through hundreds of feet of chalk. Then, they will want to inspect the septic tank. I am not worried about the building itself, but I am just a bit concerned about the small generator. In a way that is an extravagance. After all, I lived eighteen years in a farmhouse with oil lamps. But electricity will not only be convenient in that it provides light, it will also enable me to have a chest freezer in which to keep my food, but more importantly, it means I shall have an electric pump to supply water. Everyone points out that it would also mean I could have radio and even a television, though I don't imagine the reception would be much good in this place. I would not want either. They don't seem to understand what I am trying to do.

I'm not sure that I can express it in words that make any sense. All I know is that I need to be alone. It's the only way I can begin to make sense of all the confusing emotions of the past few years. Whenever I have to deal with lots of people or visit the town, I want to put my hands over my ears and shout "Stop!" That is why I find noise so distressing. That is why, most days, I set off and walk until the noise of the building is behind me. It doesn't matter whether the weather is fine or bad, up here I can sit in solitude and think." I wander, lonely as a cloud!" There are no daffodils here, or if there are I haven't found them yet, but there is plenty else to look at. I have a kind of waterproof cape and a roll of waterproof canvas which I take to sit on and in some suitable spot I sit with only the comforting sound of rain, pattering on my cape, and the quiet sounds of birds going about their business. It's like a little tent and I can sit in it for hours. On drier days I walk and explore.

I am several miles from the nearest village or town, nevertheless, there are features on these Downs which are traces of all kinds of past activity. At times in the past, I would not have been able to enjoy the same solitude. The very grass on which I walk has been turned into a magnificent lawn by centuries of grazing by flocks of sheep. I sometimes try to picture what kind of life the shepherds led. Not far from this quarry I also found a curiously lumpy little ridge. It was clearly not natural, so I fetched my spade and cut away some of the turf. I came across bricks, old bricks, smaller than modern ones. I did not take my archaeology much further, but just far enough to realise that the bricks had once formed kilns, presumably to burn the chalk and turn it into lime. It seemed unlikely that these kilns would have used coke, as more modern kilns do, so, maybe, the carbon needed was provided by charcoal. On the southern side of the slopes there are a lot of trees, including lots of hazel which has obviously been coppiced at some time in the past. I haven't explored fully yet, but I suspect I shall find clearings and evidence of charcoal burning.

In many places on the open Down there are shallow indentations, like saucers, a few feet across. These puzzled me at first so, I got my spade and attempted more archaeology. Under the thin covering of turf, I found only chalk at first. I did not understand. I squatted on my heels and looked more closely. Then I realised there was a rich seam of flint at the bottom of the depression. These little mines were probably thousands of years old. Flint and chalk go together. Many of the buildings in the Wealden below are built of flint. Flint knapping is an ancient skill. Perhaps, from the chalky earth I was looking at, men in ancient times had used deer's antlers to extract lumps of this hard material and then to sit patiently to bang it, piece on piece, skilfully to produce razor-sharp flakes.

About a mile away from the quarry, also on the southern side, I stumbled across a more recent intrusion. Buried under an accumulation of grass and turf I found the crumpled remains of an aircraft, or part of one. I knew nothing about it, but I guessed it must have crashed here during the Second World War. No doubt most of the salvageable parts had been taken away. As a boy I had witnessed the Battle of Britain at first hand. Too young fully to appreciate that these machines, and vapour trails spread across the Sussex sky, contained living people, many of whom were about to die, I had watched. My parents said little about the war, but it was evident on those occasions when the matter arose in Chapel, that they and their friends were fiercely protective of the land in which they lived, and which gave them a living. This was a feeling which was to inspire me and, I suppose, still does. The Downs symbolise "England's green and pleasant land". This feeling of national pride also attracted me to read the works of some of the people who had lived here before me. This land is mine. I share the same passionate belief in its values with those young men who died, fighting to protect it. Yes, I do miss my books.

Chris was nearly ten miles away as the crow flies, but the only access to his friend's property was on the south side of the Downs. It involved a drive of nearly twenty miles and that took him only as far as the beginning of the track. He found a reasonably good place to hide the car and then set off to walk. The going was just as bad on foot as on four wheels, uphill and badly cut up, presumably by trucks or tractors. He was both anxious about Ralph's well-being and guilty because it was nearly three months since he had last visited. He headed for the quarry. He was lucky, Ralph was hard at work on his new garden, a patch of soil, darker than the chalky stuff he had passed in the fields. Railway sleepers, lying on edge, held this soil in a rectangle. Much of it had already been worked on. Ralph was busy with a fork and a rake. He straightened up as Chris approached.

"Ralph, hello, how are you doing?"

His friend stepped down from his new garden. "Good to see you," he said, "here come into the van. You look as if you could do with a cup of tea."

This was the first time that Chris had seen the van. It was tidier than he expected. He was relieved. He had had his doubts, thinking that Ralph, with no one to look after him or even show an interest in the way he lived, might have let himself go. He had grown a beard, and he was wearing old clothes to work in, but the inside of the caravan was clean and remarkably tidy. It looked as though Ralph had at least some form of routine, self-discipline, although there was no one to whom he need be responsible. He had even washed up the dishes. From the tiny gas fridge Ralph retrieved a bottle of fresh milk.

"My project manager brings me milk every morning when he comes to work," he explained. "He leaves it at the top of the pathway there. I've got some powdered milk for emergencies."

"How are you keeping?" Chris asked.

"OK, but I'll be glad when the builders finish and leave me in peace."

Chris nodded. "What do they think about all this?" he asked.

"I have no idea," Ralph said. "I don't care one way or the other. They are getting paid. They don't need to discuss it, certainly not with me. The project manager, Graham is in charge. I don't even need to inspect it."

"Surely you must find it exciting. Don't you go and look at it every day to check on progress?"

Ralph seemed to find this a curious question. "No," he said. "I'm only impatient to see the thing finished. I know what the designs looks like. I don't want the bother of supervising it all, that's why I employ Graham."

Well, thought Chris, if this was his project, nothing would stop him watching every brick being laid, every tile being hung. He drank his tea. He had expected Ralph to ask how things were at the hospital or in town, but he said nothing.

"You're lucky to catch me today," Ralph said. "I want to get this garden going as soon as I can. The aim is to be as near self-sufficient as possible. I know quite a lot about gardening. Most days you would find the place empty. I usually take a snack or something and go for a walk to get away from all the noise."

Chris took another sip of tea and listened. Until that moment he had been quite unconscious of any sounds coming from the building site. He could hear the muffled sound of a cement mixer. As he listened, he could also just make out an occasional crash as a workman dropped something to the ground. Otherwise, it was remarkably quiet.

"It doesn't sound all that noisy to me," he said.

"I suppose not," said Ralph. "But I came here to get away from it all. That's why I walk. If you've got the energy, come with me and I'll show you what I'm talking about."

Chris followed his friend in silence as they left the quarry and headed away from the building site. Soon, even the gentle throbbing of the cement mixer faded. Within a few minutes the two men were standing on the summit. The view was impressive. There was a light wind blowing from the west, pushing clouds across the sky. Further along to the east, a little off the summit, the trees were moving in the wind. In the valley before them Chris could just make out where the town lay. He could see small fields and a solitary tractor. The only sound, however, was that of the wind in the foliage. It was certainly quiet, but Chris was used to the town, and he found the silence not to his liking. If this was what Ralph had chosen for himself, Chris was far from sure he understood.

After a while, during which time Chris had found it difficult to make conversation with his friend, they turned back and were soon comfortably settled out of the wind in the caravan.

"You're in luck," said Ralph. "I did some baking this morning." He opened a tin and took out two scones.

"Cooking? I never knew you could cook!"

"Needs must when the devil drives, as my mother used to say." Ralph produced two plates, knives and butter and made a pot of tea. Chris ate with pleasure.

"Where did you learn to cook like this?" he asked.

"I learned a lot at the farm, but it's easy enough to follow a recipe."

"Well, you certainly aren't going to starve. Does this Graham bring your food up too?"

"No, that's one of the drawbacks at the moment. I have to drive down in the Land Rover to collect supplies. That will change, I hope, when I eventually move into the cottage. You realise I'm having a generator installed?"

"Yes, it sounds like a good idea to me."

"The problem is how to muffle the noise. The little shed it will be in has to be specially built with double-skin walls."

"That sounds extravagant."

"That's what everybody says, but I wouldn't be able to stand the non-stop noise even of a small engine, night and day remember."

That sounded is very strange to Chris, but he did not comment.

"The electric light will be useful," Ralph said, "and I may well need to use hand tools for this and that."

"Hand tools? What will you need those for?"

"I spent a good many years on that farm," Ralph explained. "There are always things that need seeing to. I may need to put up fencing here and there. I'm thinking of getting half a dozen chickens and I'll need to build a roost for them. Some things I'll need to do may be quite difficult. If I do need to put up fencing, it won't be easy making holes in the chalk. There will always be things to do."

"All this is just a little reassuring," Chris said. "I had no idea how you were going to spend your time with no one to talk to."

"I'm okay looking after myself. I just don't want other people."

"I'm sorry," Chris said. "I don't really understand that. I don't think this will last all that long. I can understand your wanting time to... Well, time to recover. A lot of people would have collapsed, undergoing what you had to put up with."

"It's not always easy, Chris. Depression is like a great, heavy cloud, always hovering, always threatening to weigh me down. I just know that despair is somehow wrong. But it is difficult. As soon as I find myself slipping down into that state, I deliberately remember Gillian. She was so... so positive, so vital! She could only see happiness even at the end, even..." He stopped, unable to say more.

Chris, unsure what to do, put a sympathetic hand on his shoulder.

"Maybe I should be off," he said. "The last thing I wanted to do was to upset you."

"Chris, it was good of you to come. As for what's going on in my head, that's for me to sort out, not you. I shall always be glad to see you. But look, you've done enough walking for a townee like you. I'll take you down to your car in the old Rover. I know where most of the bad spots are, but you'll need to hang on for dear life."

Before he climbed into his car, impulsively, Chris embraced his friend. Then he muttered a goodbye and turned away. The brief allusion to Gillian remained in his head. Ralph was still grieving. Chris hoped that this project was not going to prove a dreadfully expensive mistake as seemed likely, but he also hoped that his friend would in time be ready to return to a more normal life in the community. He was, after all, only in his thirties.

Chris was not the only person worried about Ralph. The following week Ralph had to drive into town to order supplies of food and gas cylinders. He called at the post office and emptied his mailbox. He glanced at the two or three letters. They appeared to be receipts or advertising rubbish, and there was a bank statement in one fat envelope. Ralph sat in his Land Rover and opened the statement. There was a covering letter which he read. The bank manager wrote to say he would like to "have a chat." Looking at the balance on his three accounts, Ralph saw nothing to worry about. The ongoing costs of the building were high, perhaps a little higher than the original estimate, but these were essential, one-off expenses. Still, since he was already in the neighbourhood, he might as well visit the bank to see why the manager wanted a "chat." After just a few weeks living in his caravan he already felt uncomfortable, having to mix with people. He hated the jostling on the pavement, and the incessant noise of the traffic, even though it was only a small town. He pulled the hood of his jacket over his head and headed for the bank.

There were only three customers ahead of him. Ralph waited patiently and explained to the young bank clerk that he rarely came into town, but that the manager had wanted to speak to him. He gave her his name. She smiled, asked him to take a seat. She would see if the manager was free. Ralph turned towards one of the chairs.

"Ralph? Ralph Cobden, is it really?"

Disconcerted at being recognised despite his beard, Ralph looked at the speaker.

"Mr Clarke? It has been a long time," he said lamely.

"Yes, indeed. I haven't seen you since your mother's funeral. You must miss her."

"Yes." Ralph could think of nothing to add. It was now seven years since that, particular funeral. It had been doubly painful, mourning for his mother and having to speak civilly to his father's friends. Daniel had shown no wish to forgive him for what he saw as a betrayal. On his part Ralph could not forgive Daniel for his treatment of Mary, his exploitation of his son and his thick-headed opposition to Ralph's choice of career. When Daniel refused to attend his son's wedding, Ralph was at the same time relieved and offended. But now Mr Clarke's reference to his mother's funeral brought back more bitter memories, memories of another funeral, when Gillian had left him for good. At the time he had been half mad with grief, but it was a pain that was easily reawakened. For a few minutes he had to turn away and pretend to fumble with his chair.

"I didn't expect to bump into you," Mr Clarke went on, blithely unaware of the turmoil he was causing. "Someone said you had moved away."

"I'm having a cottage built for myself on Deadman's Down."

"Deadman's Down? It's a long time since I was there." Mr Clarke, to Ralph's dismay, took a seat next to him. "I can't remember anything much, no buildings that I can remember. It must be miles off the beaten track. All I do remember about it is that it's close to Druids Wood."

"That's right."

"Well, fancy bumping into you like this! It's a long time since I spent an hour teaching you how to ride a bike. Now look at you! I like your beard, by the way. Next time you're in town, you must call in at the farm for a meal. My wife would love to see you."

Ralph mumbled thanks, though he had no intention of taking up the invitation. Mr Clarke, kind, well-meaning, seemed too eager to talk. Ralph had never been good at small talk, and this was no exception. The farmer's unthinking reference to funerals had set skeletons in his head dancing as in the mediaeval Dance of Death. Ralph needed time to allow them to settle. He had little time, however, because the bank manager, Mr Grosvenor, emerged from his professional lair to welcome him. Ralph managed to stammer something to Mr Clarke before following the bank manager.

"Thank you for coming in," said Mr Grosvenor once they were settled. "You are one of our important clients, as I'm sure you realise. The reason I wanted to talk to you is that I have been looking at your accounts recently. I know that you are in the middle of building a new home for yourself. I also realise that it is more expensive than most because of its location. What worries me is that you seem to be spending a great deal of money and beginning to eat into your capital. Have you any plans for earning money to replace it? It seems that the considerable sums you received from the sale of the farm – I know that the money went to your mother in the first instance, but it has since passed on to you – and the subsequent life insurances have nearly all been – er – impacted. Much of the original cash was, of course, invested. At the very least I think we should look again at those investments, try to increase the income that way."

Ralph found it hard to give an answer. Normally good with money, since Gillian's death he had left such matters to others.

"Maybe," said the banker, "you should consult someone else, a financial adviser, an accountant. Do you know anybody?"

"Gordon Scrimshaw used to deal with the farm accounts," Ralph said.

"Ah yes, I know Mr Scrimshaw. Why don't you give him a ring?"

"I'm not on the phone," said Ralph.

Mr Grosvenor looked surprised. "Would you like to use my phone?" He said, pushing it across the desk. "I'm sure I can find his number for you."

The only way in which Ralph could arrange a meeting was for the accountant to visit him in his caravan. He agreed to talk to Gordon Scrimshaw the following week, but the prospect of allowing an intruder into his private retreat was distasteful. He thanked the bank manager and made his way as quickly as possible to the car park. He drove home without taking conscious notice of his surroundings. He was not concerned about the state of his bank balance, but the memories his encounter with Mr Clarke were painful and persistent. He recognised the symptoms of depression. He closed the door of the caravan and stretched out on the bench which served as part of the bed. He felt cold. He pulled the blanket over his shoulders and head, shutting out the light. He was overtaken by a sudden terror, and he curled up like a foetus. He awoke and threw back the covering. It was dark. He had no idea of the time. He lit one of the gas lights. It was 3 AM. He made a cup of tea and took some paracetamol. Then he opened the door and sat on the step with his tea. A little light lit up the bare, chalky earth. A few feet away he could see the edge of his garden. As yet, there were no crops. Then, at the very edge of the light, perceptible against the chalk face of the quarry he saw movement. As his eyes grew accustomed to the darkness, he realised he was looking at two deer. Since he was making no noise, they appeared to be unconscious of his presence. It was a roe deer with a fawn. They moved like dancers on their points, looking for suitable herbs to eat. Ralph watched for several minutes until they gave up and danced out of sight. He had never seen deer in the quarry before. Their beauty and timidity seemed precious, and he felt privileged to have witnessed them.

He went back inside and closed the door. He reflected for a while on his situation. His plan had always been to escape, to hide from the ties and demands of the modern world. The day's experience with the bank manager had reminded him that such a plan was impossible. He was not some mediaeval mystic, living in a cave, eating nuts and berries, and accepting the occasional offerings of alms from passers-by. He was a relatively prosperous young man in the Twentieth Century. It was the existence of such things as insurances, sales, bank loans and investments which provided him with the opportunity to live as he wished. His withdrawal from town life to his isolated retreat here depended on the existence of insurances, bank loans and investments. Just as he could never wipe out the memory of the thirty-plus years, so he could not totally ignore the rest of the world. But the skeletons still danced in his head. He did not fancy going to bed. He made more tea and made himself a sandwich, then he took his torch and walked into the warm, damp night to the top of the Down. Now he could hear some of the natural sounds. There were tiny, rustlings at grass level. Owls hooted. He remembered the barn owls he could hear from his bedroom window in the farmhouse years ago. He lay back on the grass and gazed at the stars, trying but failing to comprehend the vastness of the universe.

He stayed there a long time, hoping that the clattering of imaginary bones in his head would eventually cease. The polestar was above and in front of him as he lay. He did not look at his watch and the night passed. He became aware to his right of a slight paling of the sky. Slowly, light was returning. Immediately in front of him, the foot of the hill was in darkness still as the sun's first, weak rays picked out the solitary trees, lighting them at the top from the East, casting long shadows on the grass where cattle were already beginning to graze in the dew. He became aware of birdsong and realised it was the morning chorus, sounds he enjoyed. Ralph watched. As with the two deer, he felt privileged, humbled as a solitary spectator of something impressive and beautiful. When he finally looked at his watch it was seven o'clock. The workmen would be arriving in an hour. He stood up exercised his arms and legs to get the blood flowing and went back to the caravan.

For nearly a week Ralph's moods oscillated between depression and practical considerations, such as developing his garden. The sight of the two deer had been unexpected, but Ralph's experience on the farm made him now consider how to fence off his own, precious plot. It would mean yet another trip into town to buy chicken wire, but he would need several rolls in order to make a chicken run. For that he also needed posts and timber to build somewhere where the chicken could roost at night in safety. There were foxes about. Ralph had no illusions about foxes. They were clever. They were attractive animals to look at but they were also skilled predators, and they would create havoc among unprotected chickens. It all provided him with lots of practical work to do. Some of the work would have to wait until the cottage was complete because some of the necessary tools were in storage still.

Mr. Scrimshaw arrived as arranged. He made no comments about the unusual living conditions, simply establishing what was needed and getting Ralph to sign the necessary authority. He did not even complain at the difficult track, though Ralph noted his fee was higher than he expected. It was reassuring, after the bank manager's concern, to be told his investments were quite sound and would continue to provide steady income. Only a large, unexpected expense was likely to cause concern.

As the months passed, and the new cottage began to look less like a chaotic builder's yard, Ralph's eagerness grew. It was already clear that being even partially self-sufficient entailed much physical work. For years he had learned to rise at first light, sometimes earlier. He was now determined that, once the cottage was habitable, he would rise every day at six and spend the entire morning working on his "estate" only when the basic chores had been completed would he allow himself the luxury of retreating to his study. Exactly what he was going to do there he was as yet unsure, although he would continue with his journal. Once his precious books arrived and he had room in his library for more, he would invest in others, in the first place to research the history of this locality. He wanted to know much more about Druids Wood especially. But the flint mines, the evidence of hazel woods, and the long tradition of shepherding were all subject he would like to know more about.

Journal

I hate having to go into town. Unfortunately, I can't see myself ever being completely self-sufficient. Even growing my own food is proving far more difficult than I expected. It never occurred to me that I would have to fence off my garden, but even though I have done just that, something, probably a rabbit, managed to get in and eat all my first crop of lettuce. Maybe it was birds. Who knows? I believe wood pigeons are partial to green leaves. Anyway, I have now had to buy netting to keep out the birds as well as getting the chicken wire attached securely to the wood frame. Following my last excursion into town I am much more aware of the money I am spending. Except for the building I think I am being quite parsimonious.

That trip into town was more traumatic than I had expected. It was only good advice that I should consult an accountant, but that involved accepting a visitor into my little home – my hermit's cell. It's not that I have anything against Gordon. His advice is probably extremely sensible. He has helped me reinvest some of my dwindling capital. Once the building is complete – it is already months behind - and I am shot of the builders, the noise and the general inconvenience, my expenses will be quite low. I will need diesel for the generator and an occasional delivery of logs for the Aga. I'm not sure I can become entirely vegetarian because I don't know enough about diets. It is a possibility though. I am not entirely keen to eat meat. My garden may be crucial.

I have come to realise that I want it both ways. I want to be isolated from society in general, but I also want many of the comforts of modern living. It's only my money that will enable me to live as I wish, so I must take advice and conserve it as much as possible. Until I can get out of this caravan I cannot be entirely satisfied. Even this is better than living in a community somewhere.

That conclusion has been reinforced by the chance encounter with Mr Clarke. I had not seen him or his wife since my mother's funeral. It was not only his mention of that funeral that upset me. It was the vivid reminder of the group of people I had grown up with. He was, so to speak, a representative of the congregation of the Chapel. He and his wife were kind to me. I have known them most of my life, most intensely at pivotal moments, from their very kind gift of the bike to the practical help with the sale of the cattle. I hadn't seen Mr Clarke since then. He may not even know that I was married, nor that Gillian had died. I certainly did not want to talk about these things with him or with anyone else for that matter. People are inquisitive. They can't help themselves. They poke their noses into your business, not realising the harm they can do.

I shall never recover from the pain of the past few years. The best I can hope for is that it will become duller as time goes on. For the moment all I can do is to keep busy. Unfortunately, Autumn is now with us, and it will bring bad weather. The builders have at least got the roof on the cottage and, provided everything arrives on time, windows and doors will make the building waterproof in the next week or so. There is still a lot of work to be done, including the building for the generator and they will need to dig a large hole for the septic tank. The borehole is now functioning, although there is as yet no pump. With the building watertight they can get on with the work inside – wiring, plumbing, plastering and the installation of the staircase and a lot of carpentry. But, if the weather becomes wet, the track will become more or less impassable. The constant to-ing and fro-ing of heavy vehicles has worn the track down to the bare chalk and that, when it is wet, is as slippery as ice. It would be far too costly to repair the track as it needs. I had not foreseen any of this.

It looks as though I am going to be living in this caravan through the coming winter. I can keep it warm inside, but only at a cost and there is a problem of condensation. It would be possible to move back into town temporarily, but that is the last thing I want to do. There are compensations. On the lower slopes to the south the trees are a mixture of evergreens and native, deciduous species. They are already beginning to turn colour. The rowan trees with their vivid red berries provide a feast for the eye as well as for the birds. The red berries of the holly, too, contrast with the glossy green leaves. Walking in the woods in the rain is wonderful, gentle hissing sound and pattering of the drops on the foliage above is so soothing. I am always surprised that the birds almost ignore the rain, flying about. And on those days of really heavy rain when the builders have simply not turned up, I have perversely enjoyed their absence. This place then is really mine as it will be in due course.

Meanwhile I shall have to plan carefully to ensure that I have enough supplies to last me. The track becomes less and less manageable, even though I use the four-wheel-drive. It would be stupid to get stuck halfway up or down. Without a freezer or the power to run one it may prove very difficult. But if it is difficult for me, it will also be very difficult for anyone to visit me, whatever their reason. It's a pity that includes Chris. He is the only person who has an inkling of my true feelings, the only person whose visits are welcome.

It was to Chris that Ralph turned when it became impossible to stay in the caravan. Three weeks' continuous rain had made the track so perilous that not even the builders would risk it. They would have to use some of the broken tiles and other rubble, mixed with smaller lumps of chalk which they took from the foot of the quarry, to fill in the worst of the holes in the track. It all added to the cost. While they did so Ralph was forced to move back into the town. Chris was happy for him to use his spare bedroom for a short time, but he had made arrangements for Christmas, when he planned a family get-together. Ralph found a small and rather squalid flat. It was at least bigger than his caravan, but he spent the first few days scrubbing and cleaning. While he stayed at Chris's home, he had the place to himself because Chris was at work all day.

Ralph had brought his precious typewriter with him. For exercise he walked to the nearby park. In term time, when the children were in school, the park was almost deserted. One or two young mothers brought small children in pushchairs. There were very few adults otherwise. It was a poor substitute for the

Downs, but it afforded him a little exercise and the feel of fresh air on his face, but other visitors regarded the strange, bearded man with suspicion, especially since he pulled his hood up to hide his face when they approached him.

He took advantage of living in the town to visit the library most days. He took with him pens, pencils and a notebook and began researching the history and prehistory of the region. Here he had access to large-scale ordnance survey maps. The books he studied provided quite a lot of information. More useful were the bibliographies and Ralph noted references and books which he would order in the future.

Inevitably, there were unexpected encounters with people he knew. Such encounters were precisely why Ralph wanted to escape. They were not too frequent – the Cobdens came from a farming community. The farmers and their wives were far too busy to visit the town very often. All the same, as the weeks went by, and the dreary weather continued, Ralph's thoughts, when not preoccupied by his reading, returned to the little caravan in the quarry and the muddy building sites nearby. He pestered his project manager for reports. Progress had slowed but the improvised repairs to the track meant that they might now be able to return to the building. The weather had delayed things. The cottage would not be ready by Easter, as everyone had hoped. They would be working as hard as they could, but a more likely target would be mid to late July. It was a disappointment, although Ralph had been expecting it. The improvements to the track did at least mean that he would be able to return to the caravan. The practical problems to do with supplies persuaded him to delay his return until February. It meant he was confronted daily by signs of Christmas. Ralph had no religious belief, and he found the noisy commercialism almost offensive. Christmas as a religious festival he could understand, even though he did not any longer share the faith. It was the most serious difference between himself and Gillian. She had insisted on a church wedding, and he had fallen in with her wishes.

"I promise never to argue with you about religion," he promised her, "but I spent every

Sunday as a child listening to preachers and not believing a word of it."

"It's important to me," she said. "I love the tradition, but I also believe it. Maybe, one day, you will come to understand."

"Don't hold your breath," he said. "I don't even believe in the afterlife, let alone in the resurrection of the body."

"Well, let's not fall out about it. And think what a lovely surprise it will be one day when one of us finds the other in heaven."

They both laughed.

To turn Christmas into a pagan festival, however, seemed like an affront. He had, he realised, become thoroughly antisocial. If others found that wrong, something to be disapproved of, Ralph could only shrug. He would soon take himself off to his hermitage where he would no longer bother them and where they could no longer bother him.

Towards the end of February, the weather turned crisp and dry. With Chris's help Ralph paid a visit to the shops and stocked up with foodstuffs and several large bottles of water, since the water from the borehole had not yet been passed as drinkable. Chris followed him as far as the beginning of the track, where he left his car and climbed into the Land Rover. Even though many of the deepest holes had been filled in, the track was far worse than the first time Chris had driven this way. They arrived at the quarry. A few weeks had returned it to a derelict state. Rain had turned the floor of the quarry back into mud, not very thick, but creamy in colour and greasy to walk on.

Ralph drove as close to the caravan as he dared. Inside, everything was damp and very cold. He turned on the gas heaters until the inside of the van felt quite tropical. Chris helped him wipe down all the surfaces and the walls.

"Everything is damp," he said. "Your bedding isn't fit to sleep in."

"I'll manage." Ralph's solution was to open the windows and the doors and continue to heat the van for the next two hours. Chris helped him transfer the supplies.

"Do you think this will work?" Chris asked.

"Yes, but it's a bit like the inside of an oven already. I think we'll have to leave everything open like this while it dries out. Do you want me to take you back down to the road now?"

"I certainly don't want to leave you here until you have a reasonable bed to sleep in. Your catch pneumonia!"

Ralph shrugged. "That's what comes of living in town," he said. "Too much soft living. I'll be fine."

"Maybe. If you can bear the heat, why don't you make some tea, then, if it's okay with you, I'd like to see how far the builders have got with your cottage."

The tea was welcome, though they drank it in the Land Rover. The building site was deserted since it was Sunday. The two friends walked over the wet turf and so to the chalky desert in which the builders worked. The main walls of block work were complete, and the roof was watertight, but there were no windows or doors. The slope of the hill gave some protection from the weather which came mostly from the west, but rain had been driven through the open spaces inside. The block work formed the inner walls. The outer skin was made of flint. Chris was impressed by the skill with which these uneven pieces of stone were used to make courses of surprisingly consistent height, the flints, almost all presenting a flat surface on the outside, presumably knapped, were approximately halfway from ground to eaves. It would be a handsome building, if modest in size. The two men walked briefly inside the ground floor. There was not yet a staircase. It was hard to picture what this would be like to live in. It was, however, "coming along nicely", as Chris observed. Ralph said nothing. He was hoping that the rest of the work could be completed by summer.

Ralph led the way to the top of the hill. He did not want to talk. Chris understood his friend's wish to be silent and Ralph took pleasure and comfort from the simple companionship. They gazed for a while at the landscape. Ralph was conscious of the muted colours and the bare trees, contrasting with the scene he remembered from just a few months earlier. This was a barren time when very little grew and there was more brown earth than grass. Cattle were kept indoors. The quiet roads were completely deserted. Movement came from chimneys, thin streams of smoke which rose into the air and then disappeared, as the inhabitants sat in their sitting rooms and kitchens. Families would be recovering from their Sunday lunch.

They returned to the caravan. Ralph turned off the heating and they sat in the Land Rover for a little longer, until it was cool enough inside. Chris was going to help stow away the supplies, but Ralph said no firmly. He preferred to put things away himself. He insisted on preparing a simple meal for the two of them. He was demonstrably glad to be back. Chris said nothing, but he could not fully understand how anyone could prefer living in a small, cold, often damp caravan rather than a proper home. The small flat which Ralph had been using was cramped and lacking in light, but even that was preferable to this.

The meal over, they drank coffee. Ralph led his friend a few yards across the quarry floor to contemplate what had become of his garden. It was in a sorry state. The railway sleepers had held in the soil which was now largely waterlogged. Water seeped from underneath the sleepers, oozing a darker soil into the chalk. Some of the fence poles were now at rakish angles. Ralph would need to take them out and plant them more deeply. There was a lot to be done. It was just as well to have discovered the weakness before spring.

Ralph did not need to explain to his friend that he was thinking of the work he planned.

"If you're sure you're all right," Chris said, "can you take me down to the end of the drive? I'll be heading home."

Half an hour later Chris was back in his own vehicle, driving thoughtfully back home. He was still very worried. He no longer fully understood the friend he had known for more than a decade, a friend he thought he knew well. He was ready to accept that three deaths in a very short time, including the death of his beloved Gillian had left Ralph trying to deal with profound grief, beyond Chris's personal experience. It was the extraordinary plan to cope with it which Chris found very worrying. He knew Ralph was by nature a quiet, retiring person who loved the country. In many ways he was bookish, but to retreat as he was now doing seemed extremely unhealthy. Chris worried that he would slip further into a depressed state. Other people he had talked to shared his concern. The best that he could do was to try to visit as often as possible, but the situation made that quite difficult.

He let himself into his own, warm, little house and turned on the radio. He poured himself a stiff drink and sat a while and thought. Later, he rang another friend and arranged to meet for a drink.

Journal

What a relief to be back! I think poor Chris was a bit shocked. The van was certainly damp when we got here. Having the heating on full blast has helped, but it has used up a lot of my gas and I shall need to buy a new cylinder. It has also not done the trick properly and there is a lot of condensation to deal with. I spend a lot of time mopping up. I don't think the bed is entirely dry yet but the worst that can happen is probably that I get rheumatism.

I am more concerned with my poor garden. It is a bit like a huge, rectangular flowerpot. I should have thought about the drainage. The floor of the quarry is compacted, unlike the natural chalk outside. I can't see what I can do about it. I shall just have to wait for the soil to dry out. Given a few weeks, it might be possible to sow some seeds, but I need to get the posts properly set up and then I shall need to put some netting over the whole thing. It looks like a very big job.

The cottage does seem to be coming along but there is a great deal still to be done. I can't see it being finish before the autumn. I imagine building those flint walls can't be hurried. I am very impressed by the quality of the workmanship. There can't be that many people left with the skill these days. So, it looks as though I shall have to resign myself to another six months in this van. That means at least six months more without my books. There is no point in my ordering new ones, so I cannot do the research which I want to do.

Provided the weather is kind, I shall get on with the garden. The days are still quite short, so I can't really start before about 8 o'clock. I work for four or five hours then stop for a smack of some kind. I need to get away from the sound of the builders' cement mixer which goes on all day. So, I shall go for a walk in the afternoons. I am fascinated by Druids Wood – fascinated and strangely scared. I can't for the life of me explain why I should feel as I do. It is, after all, only a grove of trees. They are very big and obviously very old, but I can't understand why that should make them frightening. Partly it is because there are no birds. The one place you usually expect birds is in a wood, but not here. It is very dark. In fact, it is so dark nothing grows underneath the trees. I haven't visited the wood in the rain, but I suspect the canopy is so thick that no rain actually reaches the floor except by trickling down the branches and those huge, twisting trunks. And it is not silent, although there is no birdsong or other animal life. Those huge branches move, grinding one against the other. I imagine this is what it must have been like in one of those old, timber- built ships of the line. Despite this curious sense of awe which I am tempted to describe as dread, I am drawn back irresistibly. If the feeling becomes too powerful, it is only a matter of a few steps, and I can be out in the open air again.

One reason that I shall be so glad to move into the cottage is that I want to establish a daily routine for myself. I had not entirely understood how much time I would need to devote to absolutely basic chores. Preparing meals, washing up, keeping clean all takes up a lot of time. I had not thought I would need to spend time organising and collecting supplies. I don't as yet grow any of my own food, but gardening is going to take up quite a lot of my day and I shall still need to make the occasional journey to collect gas cylinders and even some foodstuffs. At the moment I feel like Robinson Crusoe, learning how to cope.

The bank manager and my accountant pestered me while I was in town. They both pointed out that the building was taking longer and costing more than I had planned. There is no real chance that I shall run out of cash altogether, but once the move is complete later this year, I plan to live much more frugally. Unfortunately, that will probably mean I need to do yet more thinking and planning. I do not want to have to commit myself to earning money if I can avoid it. That would mean regular contact with other people, something I need to avoid. People have brought me so much pain over the years. That sounds very ungrateful not only to people like Chris but even to Gillian. She brought me joy but losing her has brought me to the opposite state. The very mention of her name brings this awful mixture of remembered happiness and total despair. I want to avoid that or even the very chance of forming friendships, which are nothing but a pale imitation of love. This is all very muddled, but I just feel my best bet is to opt out of living in any kind of society as far as is possible. People have brought me nothing but loss. Yet I am well aware now after such a short experience of living here that I continue to depend on others if it's only people who bottle gas or supply food that I cannot as yet grow for myself.

I wonder how primitive people in the Iron Age coped. I wonder if they suffered the same pain from personal relationships. Were they too busy surviving? Already I begin to understand a little of the practical problems they faced. At least I have decent tools to use. I shall have a comfortable, dry house to live in, not a huge round- house in which only part of the smoke escapes through the thatch. The worst I have to deal with is a bit of mud and condensation – and that will only be for a few more months. The biggest trees I need to cut down are the little saplings, especially ash saplings which seem to spring up all at once. I don't think I would have enjoyed hunting and killing animals. And that reminds me: I must keep an eye out for deer. I haven't seen any since that one occasion, when I saw the female and her fawn. I have seen quite a lot of birds, but I don't always identify them. That's another reason I want my books.

Realistically, I now imagine it will be September at the earliest before I can move in. At least I am once more away from the town and from all those well-meaning but unwelcome acquaintances. Unlike Robinson Crusoe, I do not want to return to so-called civilization.

Chris counted out twenty-eight pills and poured them into the box, then sealed it with the printed address label. The address caught his eye, as did the name, Mrs Dorothy Clarke. He took the pills out to the counter and called her name. A small, motherly lady stepped forward, a man at her elbow. The man, obviously her husband, had an expression that suggested he was trying to remember something.

"Haven't we met somewhere?" he asked.

"Maybe," Chris said. "I thought I recognised the name, Clarke with an E. Is your farm anywhere near Cobden Farm?"

"That's it!" Arthur Clarke exclaimed in triumph, "we met at Mary Cobden's funeral."

"That was some time ago," Chris said.

"Yes, you were a friend of Ralph and his wife. What's her name?"

"Gillian," said Chris. "I'm sorry to say she passed away."

"Passed away?" Dorothy was shocked." But she was only young, a pretty girl, full of life!"

"She was. We all miss her," said Chris.

"What about Ralph? It must have come as a terrible shock to him. We've known him since he was a boy. My husband," she indicated Arthur with a nod," even taught him to ride a bike. How terrible for him to lose both his parents and his wife. Where is he now, do you know? Still local, or has he moved away? We've not seen him for a long time."

"I'm due for a break in ten minutes," Chris replied. "If you like, I can join you for a cup of tea in the café down the corridor. I can bring you up to date."

He was not sure what impelled him to suggest it. Ralph and his isolation were a persistent cause of worry. It might help to share his concern. He did not know Mr and Mrs Clarke, but his impression was of a kindly couple. They had known Ralph long before he had.

His impressions were reinforced as they sat at the small table and talked about Ralph. They described how they had known him and his parents when they all attended the same chapel. The Clarkes still attended every Sunday morning, as, they said, did many of the congregation who had known the family over the past thirty years.

"I was very fond of Mary," Mrs Clarke said. "Daniel was a little more difficult to get on with. He didn't have many interests apart from his farm."

"I never met him," Chris admitted, "but I did meet Mrs Cobden. I didn't know her very well. I liked her, though."

"The family does seem to have suffered a whole series of disasters," Arthur Clarke observed. "I know that Daniel took it very hard when Ralph refused to take on the farm. That was when he was eighteen. According to Mary, he left home and went to work on a market garden somewhere and then, of course, he did his National Service."

"That's when I first met him," said Chris.

"So, you knew him when his father was killed?"

"Yes. That was several years later. It was a pretty bizarre death."

"He trusted that bull," Arthur said. "He was quite proud of it. Unfortunately, he had this idea that dehorning cattle was unnatural. He paid dearly for that mistake."

"Mary took it quite hard," his wife said. "That would have been the only time we saw Ralph until his mother's funeral. He came back to the farm and helped his mother sell up. We bought the cattle."

"Yes, and we lost track of both of them for a while. I believe Mary bought a house in town to be close to Ralph and his wife."

"That's right," Chris confirmed. "But losing her husband and moving out of the farm took it out of her. Well, you know all that. She died two years later."

"What happened to Ralph?" Dorothy asked.

"I don't know if you know, but he was training to be a journalist."

"A journalist! And is that what he's doing now?"

"No, it didn't work out for a couple of reasons. He had to take time out to sort out all the business of selling the farm. That took a long time, then helping his mother move. The newspaper he was working for didn't take him back. He was hoping to make a living by writing as a freelance, I'm not sure how. Then, of course, his mother died, and he had to organise another funeral. He wasn't really fit to go back to work after that for a while. He was very fond of his mother, you know. And, in any case, when his mother died, he found himself all at once quite well off. She had left him all her money and that included a very big pay out from his father's life insurance as well as another one based on his mother's life."

"So, what did he do?" asked Arthur.

"I think he lost his way a bit. He and Gillian had a small house and he decided to spend some time doing it up. Gillian was working, by the way. Did I say she was a nurse? I think Ralph was trying to work out what his future would be. He had plenty of money, so didn't have to look for a job immediately and Gillian thought it would be therapeutic for him to work on the house. Then came the complete calamity: Gillian began to suffer from very severe headaches. At first, they were diagnosed as migraine, but they persisted. Finally, her condition was diagnosed as a brain tumour."

Dorothy gasped. "Oh, dear God! How absolutely dreadful! The poor girl! And poor Ralph!"

"It was a dreadful time. When she died, in some ways it was a happy release. She had begun to behave in an erratic way. Ralph was beside himself with worry then with grief. He still hasn't got over it."

"We didn't know about any of this," said Dorothy.

"I'm sorry to give you such sad news."

"So, where is Ralph living now? And what's he doing?" Arthur asked.

"You will probably understand that all this has changed him. Three funerals in a few years, not to mention the terrible experience of watching his wife lose her mind and then die, I suppose it would change anyone."

"I take it you are still in touch?"

Chris nodded. "Yes, but one of the changes has been that he doesn't like mixing with people. He tolerates me, provided I don't ask too many questions. He shut himself away. In fact, he is at the moment busy spending far too much money, having a cottage built in the back of beyond so that he can escape as far as possible."

"That doesn't sound very healthy," Arthur observed. "Where exactly is the back of beyond?"

Chris explained. He pointed out that it was almost inaccessible, and that the building itself was not yet complete. When asked for a more precise address, he explained where it was.

"I wouldn't advise you to try to visit him," he said. "His dislike of other people is almost – well, pathological."

Dorothy looked at her husband, unsure of the word. Arthur, who did not understand it either, said nothing, not willing to show his ignorance.

Chris went back to his work and the Clarkes to their car and drove home.

John Whitely had been the Minister at the Bethesda Chapel for nearly twenty years. Now in his early fifties, he was still active and much loved by his congregation. He was good at coping with bereavement, understanding, supportive and ready with practical help. He was also good with young people and keen to attract them to his congregation. He had established a youth club which met twice a week in the hall. He was unmarried, though he was physically attractive, generally a cheerful, outgoing man with a twinkle in his eye, a sign that life for him was a precious gift, a real reason to rejoice.

After the morning service it was the custom to offer tea and biscuits to any people who wanted to stay and chat. A space had been cleared at the back of the chapel. When he had shaken the hands of those who needed or wanted to go straight home, Mr Whitely returned to mingle with the others. Arthur Clarke asked if he remembered the Cobdens.

"Yes, of course. Poor Daniel! That was a terrible accident. And Mary – she was a lovely lady – she didn't last long after her husband died. Very sad."

"Do you remember their son?"

"Ralph, wasn't it? A bright boy. He went on to Oxford. He drifted away from the church, I think. I vaguely remember meeting his wife, a doctor, wasn't she? Pretty girl."

"So, you don't know she died."

"No! That's truly tragic."

"A brain tumour, we were told. She was a nurse."

Dorothy and her husband told the Minister how they had met a close friend of Ralph Cobden. From what they had learned Ralph was badly affected by the death of his young wife. They explained that his behaviour was eccentric: he had inherited a goodly sum, they said, and looked like wasting much of it, building a cottage miles from anywhere. John Whitely though in biblical terms that Ralph had fled into the wilderness. He asked if the Clarkes knew where Ralph was.

"From what his friend told us, said Arthur, "I don't think he'd welcome a visit, not even from you. No offense!"

"None taken. I feel responsible, all the same. Ralph was part of our congregation."

His attention was taken by another person and the subject was dropped. Mary was worried that their disclosure might lead to unwanted consequences. She was to be proved right.

John Whitely was a practical Christian. He believed strongly in the power of prayer, but he also believed that God helps those who help themselves. He remembered to pray for Ralph Cobden every night as well as including him in the list of named persons at the services he took. He was full of compassion at the thought of this young man who had suffered three losses in just a few years. If, as Arthur and Dorothy Clarke reported, his reaction had been to withdraw from the world, the Minister could understand but not agree this was the best solution to his grief. Ralph Cobden was still, in his eyes, a member of the congregation. He had been unable to offer him the support he gave to other people when they were bereaved. His conscience nagged him. Thinking about this, he began to consider an idea. If the mountain wouldn't come to Mohammed, he told himself, perhaps Mohammed should visit the mountain, though he smiled at the confusion of religious images.

Two weeks after his conversation with the Clarkes, he put his idea into practice. He addressed himself first to members of the Youth Club. Later he also asked older members of his congregation, choosing those who were relatively fit. He told them that he wanted to raise funds for the Methodist Mission in Zambia and asked if the members of the congregation would join him on a sponsored walk. He would hire a large minibus to take them to the starting point a few miles away in the Downs. The suggestion was met with surprise, but the Minister was a very persuasive person and, over the next four weeks he recruited sixteen people, ten of them were members of the Youth Club, the other six were three young couples.

The minibus stopped at the beginning of the track which led to Ralph Cobden's property. John Whitely reassured them that the going would be much better once they reach the end of this track. Even on foot it was hard going at first, and the walkers were obliged to skirt round the worst parts in single file. They were beginning to wonder what they had let themselves in for when they reached the point where they could see workmen on scaffolding, building the new cottage.

One of the builders came to meet them.

"This is private property," he said.

"Ah," said John Whitely, "so sorry to intrude. We are on a sponsored walk for charity, so we are just passing through. I believe we know the owner, Ralph Cobden. Is he here? It would be nice to say hello before we moved on."

Graham was quite sure Ralph would not like to see them.

"Mr Cobden," "he said, "is not here as you can see, and the building is not complete, so, for the moment, he lives in a caravan in the old quarry. But he does not welcome visitors."

"Thank you very much," said Mr Whitely. "In that case, we will leave you alone."

Telling the group to follow him, to Graham's dismay, he headed across the grass towards the quarry. Graham assumed he had mistaken the direction and shouted after him, but the Minister affected not to hear him and in just a matter of moments all seventeen cheerfully chattering ramblers found themselves in a small flat area in front of a caravan, beyond which rose the short face of the disused chalk quarry. To their left, a structure of tall posts supported a stretch of chicken wire, and beyond that was the beginnings of a garden. Ralph Cobden, bearded, dishevelled, wearing old and dirty clothes, stared at them.

"This is private property," he shouted. He waved his arms as though to shoo them off like a flock of sheep. All, except for the Minister, were embarrassed and began to turn back, but John Whitely did not move.

"Ralph? Ralph Cobden? It's Mr Whitely, the Minister. You remember me, surely? We are just on a ramble."

Ralph realised immediately that the choice of his quarry as a starting point for a ramble could not possibly be accidental, was growing rapidly very angry.

"The old path to the Downs," he said, "is that way." He pointed. "Please don't come back this way. It won't take you far out of your way. I do not welcome visitors."

The Minister still held his ground, but the rest of the flock were already heading in the direction of the pointing arm. This very strange man with his filthy, old clothes, long hair, and straggly beard, looked mad. Some of the younger walkers felt more than a little scared, though they would never admit it. The were not prepared for this encounter. The rough track had been unexpected; what they had expected was a pleasant walk on the soft turf from where they could enjoy good views as well as the companionship of the rest of the party. Confronted with this strange, shouting, hostile figure, they were keen to get away. Only John Whitely remained and tried to engage him in a conversation. He tried but was unsuccessful.

"Yes, I recognise you, Mr Whitely. I left your church several years ago. Please don't bring it back to me here. The path you want is that way."

John Whitely was shocked. This uncouth character was nothing like the Ralph Cobden he remembered. This was clearly not the time nor the place to engage him in any kind of conversation. His appearance and his behaviour were both unexpected and hostile. He wondered if the man was losing his mind. Perhaps choosing to live in this remote spot was itself a sign that he was mad and needed help.

"I'm sorry we intruded," he said. "We'll find another way back. We shall be praying for you. God bless you."

There was no reply. Ralph stared as the Minister followed his flock back towards the original path. He stared until the last man disappeared from view. He was leaning on his spade, his hands gripping the handle so tightly they were white. The intrusion had shaken him, and he felt not only angry, but insecure and vulnerable. Even here, miles from civilisation, people pursued him, wanted to drive him back into meaningless conversations. He wanted no part of it. Why could they not understand? He thrust the spade deeply into the soil of the garden, stepped out of the crude gate and sought the sanctuary of his caravan. He made himself a mug of tea after closing the door and sat in the armchair. He was shaking. He remained there for the rest of the day. He could not be sure they would not return. His anger grew, mingled with resentment. What motivated the Minister to bring a whole crowd of visitors? He wanted nothing more to do with him and his like. A crowd of do-gooders, worshipping a meaningless God, a god of love that watched his creatures suffer and die. It was not for him, and he resented someone trying to accept such nonsense. Meanwhile, why had Graham not managed to stop them? He knew the last thing he, Ralph, wanted was to be disturbed. The only person in the least welcome was Chris, but even Chris would be unwelcome if at any time he tried to drag him back into the world he was getting away from.

Journal

When Graham came to see me in the quarry this morning, I knew there was a problem. He has been very good about not contacting me, so this was likely to be an emergency of some kind. It should not have been a surprise. I knew the track was in a bad way. Even without rain, the trucks had made the ruts much worse. No, Graham told me, it had reached the point where it was virtually impassable. I haven't tried to drive down for the past three weeks. I knew it was bad then, but Graham told me his drivers now refused to use it unless it was repaired. He looked extremely uncomfortable, telling me this. Of course, it was a serious blow. It's not just that I still need to get some important supplies delivered, things like the new kitchen fitments, including the Aga, and all the materials for the bathroom as well as the material for the generator. And the builders themselves have to get here. I told Graham not to apologise. It wasn't his fault, and it was a problem we should have foreseen. I asked him if he had any suggestions. He said that to put in a substantial road would cost half a million.

It was beginning to rain, just a fine drizzle, but there was nothing for it, I had to ask him to come into the caravan. He looked as uncomfortable as I felt. However, this was a serious emergency I asked if he had any other ideas. He said there were two problems, not just one. The first was finding suitable material to make good the worst parts of the track (five or six places). The second was getting hold of suitable equipment to compress it. Ideally, a good track needed hard-core underneath a water repellent top surface of tarmac or something similar. That would be extremely expensive, beyond anything I could afford. I asked if there was any way we could patch it up as a temporary remedy. There was a possible answer, he said, but he wouldn't guarantee it would do the trick, and it would probably not last very long. I said it only needed to last long enough to complete all the building. He was not even sure it would do that. I asked him to be more definite. He said the material might be right on hand. We had run out of hard-core, he said, but it might be possible to fill up the worst of the halls and ruts with chalk. We were sitting in a small quarry. If we could use the chalk somehow, we would need to compress it. It was even possible, he said, to hire a small road roller, though he doubted whether it would be up to the job. Then he came up with an original thought: a farmer he knew had recently invested in a second-hand crawler tractor. It was like a small bulldozer, tracked. The farmer had bought it because the tracks spread the weight. Exactly how heavy it was, Graham did not know, but provided the chalk was not too lumpy, it might do the trick for the time being. He could probably negotiate the hire of this tractor. What did I think?

"Any port in a storm", I told him." But how do we dig out the chalk to begin with, and how can we carry it to the track"? It was at least an idea worth trying. I told myself that if this all worked, I would reward Graham with a large bonus. I had hired him because he had a great reputation as a fixer. I asked him to carry on, see if he could make this plan work. We were really in a very difficult place. If we couldn't repair the track, the building would never be finished and, apart from the huge waste of money, my plan for "The Hermitage" would come to nothing. If Graham could somehow get this plan working, one of the first things to do

would be to move the caravan out of the quarry.

There was no flat ground elsewhere. The best I could find was a slightly bumpy area of grass below the ridge that hid the old kilns. It was far from ideal, being exposed, and there would be inevitable noise from the quarry and eventually from whatever truck was used to carry the chalk. The tractor would also be noisy, I assumed. I was right about that. The crawler was a powerful beast, much smaller than I had imagined, steered by two levers. Graham managed to persuade one of the drivers to make one last trip from the road to the quarry. Even if we had splashed out on the hire of a mechanical digger, we could not have brought it up the track, so the work had to be done entirely by hand. I agreed to pay double wages because the men were obliged to work like the navigators of old who had dug miles of canals. Using picks and shovels they dug away the surface of the quarry. Large rocks were then broken up when possible. The men shovelled the chalk onto the back of the small truck and, starting at the top of the track, began to fill the worst of the holes. Once this operation was completed for about fifteen yards, the crawler crunched its way across, backwards and forwards. It was a very slow business. It was to take months.

Faced with so many unexpected challenges, Ralph's resolution wavered. It proved impossible to move the caravan without damaging it. The best that could be managed was to move it to one side of the track at the entrance to the quarry. It was not a position Ralph could live with. With great reluctance he decided he would once more have to retreat to the town. Even that was a major problem. He was quite sure that Chris would let him stay for a short time, but the track was impassable, or very nearly. Even his sturdy Land Rover was in danger of suffering major damage.

The Sunday before he moved would be the last for several months. He was profoundly depressed all day. He even questioned the original decision to move here. It was certainly not working out as planned. The entire project had been beset by practical difficulties. It would take several months to deal with the track and no further progress would be made on the cottage in the meantime. He would have to spend a second winter in the town. So far, even the time he had spent in the caravan had not been peaceful and quiet. The building of the cottage and the consequent to-ing and fro-ing of the lorries bringing supplies strained his nerves.

The unexpected and unwanted visit by the Minister had been a shock. It was obvious to Ralph that the "ramble" was an excuse for Mr Whitely to pay him a visit. Someone must have told him where to look. Very few people knew where the cottage was. It was extremely unlikely that the solicitor, the bank manager or even the estate agent would pass on the address. That left only Chris. It seemed unlikely, but he could think of no other explanation. If it were true, and he would ask his friend, when he saw him, then Ralph would be extremely angry and betrayed.

The building site was silent. He took a flask of tea and some food and set off, walking westward. The fresh air, the bird song, and the absence of anybody as far as he could see did little to cheer him. This project, which he had entered into in the belief it would allow him space, both literally and metaphorically, had simply been a source of yet more stress. He had hoped that a long period of isolation in which the peace of this beautiful landscape would seep into his soul, would give him room to think. Life had not only battered him; it had also left him confused. Religious people, like John Whitely, had a ready-made explanation for the way the world was. Anything that Ralph found puzzling they simply put down to the will of God. Without God, however, Ralph wanted to work out for himself what, if anything, was the purpose of it all. He strode along on the silent turf until he was approaching the path to Druids Wood once more. He entered the trees. There was very little light here and there was a noticeable chill. He sat on one of the huge branches, just inches off the ground and poured himself a mug of tea. He spilled some on the ground and immediately thought of the accident as a libation to some of the ancient gods that appeared to haunt this place. He shivered. The depression which he felt like a physical burden was stronger than ever. He tried to reason himself into a better mood, telling himself that he had much to be thankful for. Despite his expenditure on the project, he still had enough money. He would have a purpose-built home in one of the loveliest parts of the country. But he knew he was only fooling himself: none of these things mattered: he had lost Gillian. He wept.

He stood up and shouted loud, angry, helpless, curses until he had to stop and give way to a fit of coughing. He leaned against the large trunk and looked around. His shouting had had no effect since there were no birds in the wood. These great trees which had lived for centuries were entirely without feeling. He turned and made his way hastily into the sunlight and retraced his steps to the top of the hill where he sat and stared at the landscape. Nothing moved. He was without purpose. He closed his eyes. Immediately an image of the large yew tree presented itself and he remembered reading that a man had hanged himself on such a tree. He shivered. Yew trees, he remembered, had always been associated with death. He did not know if that was because they were planted in graveyards or if it was the reason they were to be found there. But the last thing he wanted or needed was to think about death. He jumped to his feet and walked briskly for half an hour, then turned and headed back to his caravan to prepare it for his move the next day.

No further progress on the cottage itself was possible. It was nearing the end of September before the track would be complete. He would have to spend another winter elsewhere. Some of the tradespeople, notably the electricians and the plumbers, found other contracts which they would need to complete. And every delay added to the cost. Ralph had begun this venture without much thought for the overall cost. Other people had raised the question, but he had shrugged them off. However, the additional cost involved in repairing the track was beginning to worry him now. He had to pay for somewhere to live for another winter.

Chris was surprised when Ralph turned up, unannounced, but he was happy to make over the use of his spare room. He found Ralph sitting in his Land Rover on his drive when he got home from work one evening. He walked past the cab and raised a hand in salute as he put the key in the lock. Ralph got out of his vehicle. He was carrying a small bag of belongings, but Chris was shocked by his appearance. The two men had not met for several weeks. In that time Ralph's hair and beard had grown. He looked decidedly unkempt. His clothes were stained and worn. Chris wondered if his friend had given up even the most rudimentary attempt to look after himself. He shook hands and ushered him in. He noted that Ralph's clothes had the characteristic smell of someone who had not washed or cleaned them for a while.

"I imagine you've come to stay," he said. "I'll need to make the bed up. Why don't you enjoy a bit of luxury while you wait, have a bath?"

It had not occurred to Ralph that he was unpresentable. He did not have a mirror in the caravan. He knew his hair was growing long, as was his beard. He used a comb every morning, and at weekends, when there was no one about, he had fixed up a crude shower outside. On wet weekends he made do with a strip wash. It did not occur to him that his clothes needed cleaning, other than his shirts and underwear which he washed as best he could in the small sink. Chris's suggestion that he should have a bath made him realise that he had perhaps not taken too much care. A bath, in any case, would be welcome. As he ran the water, he caught sight of himself in the mirror for the first time. His beard reached halfway down his chest and was in need of a serious trim. He was less concerned about his hair, which hung down his back. He relaxed in the warm water and felt exhausted.

When he dressed in the same clothes and went downstairs, Chris was busy preparing a meal. They ate in the living room without speaking much, but afterwards they sat in easy chairs with a mug of coffee each. Chris seemed keen to talk. Ralph would have preferred to sit in silence, though he also wanted to know if it was his friend who had directed Mr Whitely to the caravan. He would bring the subject up in the morning. For the moment he was glad of a bed for a few nights while he found somewhere else.

But Chris was looking at him with a strange expression. Ralph thought he could see a kind of pity, or was it distaste?

"Ralph," Chris said, "I'll be blunt. We've known each other a good few years now. You look terrible. I realise you're living in a cramped space, but, well, you look like a Hippy. I've never seen you wearing clothes like these, either. You need to take your clothes to a cleaner."

"Does it matter?"

"Yes, I think it does. You look like a tramp. That suggests you are losing self-respect and that worries me."

"You're right. I don't much care. I haven't got any clean clothes, anyway. I suppose I could buy some, but I really don't fancy shopping. To be completely honest, Chris, I don't know that I could face it."

"You and I are about the same size. Why don't you grab some of my stuff for now? It isn't good for you to let yourself go like this. And you really need to visit a barber."

"A barber?"

"Just think what the old Sergeant Major would say,' Get your hair cut! You're a disgrace!'"

Chris said this with a smile, trying to soften the criticism, but Ralph stared back at him without blinking. "No barbers," he said. "If it bothers you so much, find some scissors and hack it off."

"OK. In the kitchen. I'll find you some clean clothes. You know what they say, cleanliness is next to godliness."

Ralph was unimpressed but fell in with his friend's suggestion. Half an hour later the kitchen floor was covered in hair. Ralph's beard was several inches shorter and no longer ragged. He wore clean jeans and tee shirt. He helped Chris clear up, then resumed his place in the living room. The transformation met won his friend's approval, but it had made no difference to Ralph's mood. He still did not care what he looked like, nor was he concerned what other people thought of him.

Journal

Well, here I am again, back in this miserable, little town. In some ways I am lucky to find somewhere, I suppose. I'm probably paying an extortionate rent. I have an upstairs flat. It is furnished and has everything I need – not that I need very much. The flat beneath me is occupied by a couple who seem to be out at work all day. Unfortunately, when they come home, they are noisy. As soon as they are indoors, they play music or turn on the television set. The floors are not very soundproof, so the evenings could be torment for me. During the day it is quiet, although the sitting room overlooks the main street, so I could not at first have the windows open. I hate noise. After the peace and quiet of the quarry, this was s at times almost unbearable until I found a way to shut out the noise.

I was glad to leave Chris's house. From the start he wanted to change me. I went along with him to begin with, borrowing some of his clothes, even allowing him to cut my beard and my hair. But he left me in no doubt that he disapproved of my plans and of my lifestyle. I lay in bed that first night and thought carefully about what I was going to do next. I used his phone the next day to contact one or two people, first and foremost was the estate agent. I explained that I was not over-concerned with costs, but I needed somewhere to stay for a few months, probably until March next year. He told me I might be in luck: he had that very day been told of a flat that would be unexpectedly vacated in the next week. I rang the local outfitters and ask them to deliver two pairs of trousers, six shirts, a pullover, underwear, and socks. I would pay by cheque. They were probably glad of the business because they went along with it. Fortunately, everything fitted.

When Chris got home from work that evening, I rustled up a meal for both of us. He was still keen to talk. I did not want to listen to a whole series of arguments in which he would try to persuade me to give up my plans. Apart from anything else, it was now too late. The cottage, although not finished, was well on the way. As Chris himself had pointed out before, it was not only virtually inaccessible, but it would also be unsellable. All the money I had spent and was still spending would be completely wasted. In any case, I really did not want to give up. Once all the building was complete and the track was more or less passable, I wanted to move in. This flat, or something like it in turn would not distance me from people, from interruptions, from interference. Even Chris's interference was irritating. I needed to be on my own.

My determination was made complete when that evening I asked Chris outright if it was he who had told the Minister where I lived. I told him of the unexpected, intrusive visit of the so-called rambling group. There were only one or two people who knew where my caravan was parked. He was one of them. No, Chris said, he had not spoken to the Minister. Then, after sitting for a few minutes, trying to work it out, he admitted speaking to Mr and Mrs Clarke. Since they were regular chapel- goers, I didn't have to be a genius to work out what had happened. I was furious. Chris and I had been friends ever since those early days in the Army. We had formed the habit even then of watching each other's backs. There was an unspoken bond of loyalty between us. Now Chris, who was outspoken in his criticism of my whole building project, had interfered in my life, passing on information which would inevitably lead to a gross intrusion on my privacy. To make matters worse, he appeared not to understand how I felt, saying that his indiscretion had been nothing less than an attempt to help me. It was like a believer telling nonbeliever to repent and re-join the congregation. I could not forgive him, and I told him so. I would leave the following day, I said, and this time I expected to be left alone. I did not tell him where I intended to go, indeed, I was not entirely sure myself. Chris was very upset, still not understanding what he had done.

The next day I booked into a small guest house on the outskirts of the town. I told no one where I was. I did not leave the guest house for three days, after which time I moved in here. My Land Rover is parked at the back, out of sight. Chris is at work all day, so there is little chance of my running into him, provided I stay indoors at the weekend. That suits me. Four doors down from here there is a small pharmacy. I had a bright idea. I bought some earplugs. I was surprised at the wide selection available, so I bought three different kinds. I also bought some dark glasses so, with a cap which I pull over my eyes, dark glasses, and earplugs, I found it tolerable to venture into the street when necessary.

Perhaps the only argument in favour of living in a town lies in convenience. It is very simple to visit my bank to draw cash when I need it. Groceries, including milk and dairy products and bread, are readily available. All I have to do is to carry them home in a shopping bag. I am, so to speak, hidden behind my glasses, my beard, and even shielded from the many noises that would normally distress me. I am a non-person. No one gives me a second glance. That suits me. It also enables me to walk a little further afield as far as the town library. There I can sit, incognito, undisturbed by anyone. I have discovered that there are numerous individuals who use the library in a similar way. Every day I see the same six or seven individuals, mostly older people, who arrive, pick up a newspaper, magazine or a book and settle in silence. At first, I did not understand why they came, then I realised the library was quiet, anonymous and warm. These people had more in common with me than Chris.

I made a beeline for the shelves on which I found books about the area. It took a while for me to locate authoritative information about the Druids. My visits to Druids Wood remained vivid in my mind. I was at once fascinated and slightly scared by the numinous atmosphere of those ancient yews. I was disappointed and surprised at first at the paucity of information. Then I realised that the Druids kept no written records. Most of the information seemed to be taken from Julius Caesar's account of ancient Gaul. I have no way of knowing how accurate that account is nor whether it applies to the ancient Britons. All I learned was that Druids were a kind of priest caste. They were the chiefs, the leaders. The Druids it was that set the rules for the Celtic community. They acted as judges. There were suggestions that part of their religious belief involved sacrifice and there was also a suggestion that human sacrifice might be involved. The most savage and vivid example was the making of large, wicker structures in human form in which the victims were imprisoned. When complete, the structure was then set alight. Reading this sent a shiver down my spine. However, the Druids will also be providers of learning, particularly for young men who joined to study natural sciences, philosophy, and poetry. The poetry was extremely important because it was the major means of remembering. The folklore was therefore preserved orally and that, presumably, is why it faded away as the Romans invaded most of Europe, making it part of their own empire. Druidism was banned and Christianity took its place.

And that was almost all I learned of the ancient Druids. The Celtic fringes of the UK – Ireland, Wales, Scotland, and Cornwall – witnessed a revival of interest in pre-Christian traditions as well as some mediaeval history during the 19th century. The Romantics glamorised it. They probably painted an entirely false picture too. According to Caesar the Druids held annual gatherings in open spaces in the middle of a forest. This information did not match my understanding of the Druid' Wood, where the ominous feeling hung like a miasma out of the darkness of the canopy. That could surely not be entirely my imagination. As for human sacrifices, that was something I could probably never know, nor did I want to, though echoes of the ritual could still be found in some of the more remote parts of Britain.

My visits to the library filled many days. Once I was in my seat, a collection of books in front of me, together with a notebook and pencil (no pens were allowed), my attention was given to my studies. The library was silent, except for the occasional shuffling of feet, but I had my earplugs. Head down to focus on my books, I was almost totally shielded from prying eyes. In fact, this was probably the safest I felt all the weary months I was forced to live surrounded by people.

Ralph continued to use his post office box so as not to disclose his address to anyone, even the bank or the solicitor. Almost all the correspondence consisted of official letters, invoices, statements, and receipts and needed no response. Progress on the repairs to the track, however, required a more direct method of communication. Once a week he drove at dawn out to the road end in time to intercept Graham Morton as he arrived. In this way he learned that progress was slow but steady. Much of the chalk took the form of large lumps, too big to be handled and too hard to be broken up easily. Between the large pieces the fragments were usable, but it involved a great deal of hard, manual labour. The crawler tractor was not always successful in crushing some of these lumps which then had to be broken up using a heavy, metal sledgehammer and steel chisels. Two of the original six men gave up, slowing the progress further. Graham had been obliged to offer the remaining four even higher wages to continue. Recognising Ralph's determination to see the matter through, Graham took care not to make any negative comment. But he reported that the work on the track would probably be complete before Christmas. This was not to Ralph's liking, but Graham pointed out that he would find it difficult to recruit workers even when the weather was fine and dry.

So it was with mixed feelings that Ralph bumped and jolted his way along the refurbished track as far as the caravan. He looked briefly into the quarry. His garden had been totally crushed. Some of the soil remained, but the fencing needed complete replacement. The floor of the quarry was now littered with large lumps of chalk, far too big to be moved by hand. The caravan was undamaged, but it was not on a flat piece of land and would have to be repositioned. It would also need cleaning inside and out.

Ralph walked the short distance to the building site. Nothing there had changed. Before work on the house had stopped, Graham had ensured that it was as secure as his skill could make it. Doors and windows were covered with board which would withstand any further storms. He turned away, scraped the mud from his boots, and drove across the uneven surface to the road.

When Ralph Cobden had refused, stubbornly, all his financial advisers' efforts to dissuade him from buying a derelict property, the estate agent, who was astonished and grateful to get rid of the property in question, suggested an architect, and the architect in turn recommended Graham Morton as a project manager. Graham Morton had spent his working life in the building trade.

Ralph took an instant liking to the man. He had all the necessary skills to rebuild the cottage, including knowledge of building in flint.

Ralph Cobden, despite the obvious difficulties, insisted that he wanted to go ahead, whatever the cost. He said that he wanted only initial consultation about the design of the new building. He would pass over all control of the practical problems to the project manager. He knew this was a big responsibility, a fact which we would be reflected in the terms of the contract.

When the track became impassable, the project had to come to a halt. If this was an industrial undertaking, the company concerned would not only have foreseen the problem, but they would also have included in their costings the considerable price of building a private road. But even Ralph Compton would not pay hundreds of thousands of pounds for a new road. Apart from the enormous cost, and new road would provide too easy access to casual visitors, perhaps it would invite visitors to the Downs, ramblers who arrived by car, to make their way from the main road up to the quarry or at least close to the new house.

Though most of the letters in the post office box were official, some official information arrived in thinner, smaller envelopes. Among these, soon after Ralph had moved into the flat, was a letter from Chris. Despite the temptation to throw it straight into the wastepaper basket, he opened it.

Dear Ralph,

I'm so sorry we parted on such bad terms. I hope we can repair the damage somehow, but it's difficult when I don't know where you are. I'm not even sure this letter will reach you. After so many years we surely can't allow our friendship to end like this. I'm not even clear what I've done to offend you so badly. I had no idea that where you were living was to be kept a complete secret from everybody. And I did not expect the Clarkes to pass on the information to the Minister at the church. I'm sure their intentions were honest. Everybody involved wants to help you. We are all concerned for you. And I hope you'll forgive me as an old friend if I say that your behaviour, ever since you lost Gillian, has been unpredictable. Everyone understands her death must have been devastating for you and grief affects everybody differently. As for me, I have been very worried by your decision to live like a hermit in the depths of the country. Quite apart from the loneliness and isolation, there will surely be practical problems. What happens if you have a bad accident, for example? You said that you don't even intend to have a phone. Of course, I'm worried about you. When I told you that, your reaction seems to be that I am interfering. And, in addition to all that, I miss your friendship. Please let me know where you are or at least how I can contact you. I am truly worried on your behalf.

Chris

Ralph tore up the letter. He did not want anyone, even Chris coming to him with advice or criticism. He was more than ever convinced that his decision to live in his hermitage was the right thing. Chris did not understand any better than anyone else. So far other people either disappointed him or opposed his wishes. Nature alone seemed to offer solace. He was not foolish enough to ascribe any consciousness or purpose to nature, though he could at times understand how people like the Druids worshipped trees or the sun or the sea. Nature did not criticise. It simply *was*.

When he looked back, he realised that he had spent his childhood years as an unpaid farm worker. His father had used him rather than loved him. Not for the first time he felt huge regret that he had never been able, nor made the time to speak to his father about such things before he had been killed by Caesar. By way of contrast, he had always been able to show his mother the affection he felt for her. He had not helped her, however, by breaking off relations with Daniel. Ralph blamed himself for much of the unhappiness that his mother had experienced before she, too, died too early. As for Gillian, their passion still raged when she first fell ill. Her loss was the ultimate cruelty. The loss of Chris's friendship was insignificant in comparison.

He was unable to think further. Thoughts were overwhelmed by strong feelings. He made his way to the bedroom where he collapsed, literally prostrate with grief. He lay there, unthinking, until the fading light from the window made him realise several hours had passed. When he got up, he felt exhausted. He was unable to return to any of his previous thinking, instead he felt numb. He wondered briefly if death was like this. It was not too bad. It was a state in which he could exist but one which could easily be destroyed by contact with other people. Yes, he would continue to exist in this numb state until the cottage was at last ready for him.

Chris was not surprised that his letter was ignored. He could not even be sure that it had reached its destination. Ralph had obviously left the caravan, but where he was now living remained a mystery. The routine work at the pharmacy left Chris with little time for himself. Theoretically, he had every other weekend free as well as one day per week. But that was theoretical: the pharmacist who was to relieve him was not a permanent employee, and there were some weeks when Chris was entirely on his own. He could not count on having a free day. So, although he remained anxious as well as upset by Ralph's abrupt disappearance, he was unable to track him down when there was no reply to his letter. In fact, it was six weeks after the quarrel that he drove out to the cottage. With difficulty he walked up the uneven track until he reached the point where he came face-to-face with a large, tracked vehicle which was crunching its way across chalk. Carefully, he made his way around the edges of the now white track. It was obvious enough what was going on, much of the track have been turned into a wider, flatter road and the verges had also been showered with bits of broken chalk. It was, thought Chris, a desecration done in Ralph's name. He would surely be dismayed.

He arrived at the quarry. The caravan had been moved a little distance and now stood on the edge of the track. It was tilted to one side and uninhabitable. Inside the quarry the ground was badly churned up where this crawler had done its worst. A small truck stood close to the quarry face where four men were busy. Two of them were hacking at the face with pickaxes while the other two were shovelling chalk into the truck. It looked like a team of convicts doing hard labour. And around the sides of the quarry there were several very large pieces of rock, far too big for anyone to lift onto the truck. The tractor had doubtless been used to manoeuvre them into two semicircles. They looked for all the world like tombstones that had been removed from an overgrown graveyard and placed where people could look at them. It was not a scene Chris wanted to watch for long. This was certainly not where Ralph would come to find refuge. He would probably be appalled at the devastation when he finally came back. Chris took a very quick look at the state of the half- built cottage, noted that it looked secure, calculated that it was in any case far enough off the beaten track to avoid the depredations of vandals, and made his way back to his car.

He had not really expected to find Ralph there. He could do nothing more.

November arrived, bringing a period of heavy rain. When it eased in early December at last, Chris returned to the building site. He arrived at the beginning of the track and found a reasonably flat parking place. The road was stained white where the rain had washed off the surface of the track and ran in a stream down the slope. The track itself had been finished. The surface was still quite uneven, but there seemed to be no ruts, nor holes. The chalk had been partially crushed and showed the marks left by the tracks of the crawler. It was, nevertheless, a distressing sight. The lane was now wider, presumably to allow access by trucks since there was still work to be done on the cottage itself. Chris had noticed that doors and windows were still boarded up and, although he was not entirely familiar with building practices, he assumed there would be most of the interior work to be done only after the building was watertight. If he was right, there would be doors, windows, major carpentry, including a staircase, possibly even floorboards, maybe interior walls, possibly plumbing, electricity, interior partitions, kitchen, and bathroom fitments, all of which would have to be brought by lorry and installed. And had Ralph not said something about installing a generator? Where was that going to be housed? There was clearly no likelihood that he would be able to move in for many months. The caravan was still sitting at an angle. Once more Chris made his way back to the road where he had parked the car. He walks down the new surface, taking care to avoid the bumps which could easily trip someone on foot. As it was, the wet chalk was greasy, and his boots were soon clogged with a layer of chalky mud. He found a clean patch of grass to wipe off most of it before driving bank to turn in poor spirits.

He was not to know he missed Ralph by two days. Ralph had arranged to meet Graham on site once a month. If Chris had chosen the same day, he would have witnessed a display of intense anger. The sight of a wide stretch of barren chalk, seemingly carved into the grass that lay on either side, was like a cruel wound. Ralph, whose mood had recently stabilised and lacked any sign of interest in his surroundings, was roused to deep anger.

"What in God's name have you done?" he shouted at the project manager.

"It will look better in time," Graham replied. He was taken aback by Ralph's fury. Up to this moment there had been no arguments to speak of. The only time he had seen Ralph angry had been when the ramblers had visited the quarry.

"This is so – so bloody ugly!" Ralph dismissed Graham's reply. "You can't leave it like this. It's hideous. It's like – like a huge wound, white, not red. It looks as though the very earth is bleeding. You've got to do something about it."

Graham said nothing at first and the two men stood on the stained road, staring at the wide, white river. True, Graham acknowledged, it looked ugly, but the purpose of the exercise was to allow lorries to reach the building site. If the mad man wanted to build up there, he, Graham, had to get stuff delivered. It had required a lot of organising to get this track done. He had already come close to spending all the agreed budget. A proper road, with a hardcore foundation and a waterproof surface, would have cost a fortune. This was a pretty good compromise. It would allow him to finish the build.

"Can't you cover all this damned chalk with something?"

"I'm not a road builder," said Graham. "This was the best compromise I could come up with."

"Change it! We can't leave it like this."

"We've already spent the budget we agreed. There's no money for cosmetics."

"How much more will it cost?"

Graham noted the use of 'will' rather than 'would'. "I can't say off the top of my head. It will depend on what we can do. If we sub-contract, I have no idea."

"Find out, and quickly."

"We're a long way behind schedule, too," said Graham. "We didn't foresee the problem with the road. I shall have to reorganise the deliveries. There's also a problem with the tradespeople who will be working on other projects."

"That's why we hired you," said Ralph. "Sort it out"

"It would be a lot easier, if I could phone you," said Graham. "The arrangement was that I was to go ahead and not consult you, but that doesn't work. We could be looking at a lot more expenditure and I shall need your say-so."

He was beginning to feel exasperated at this extraordinary, uncommunicative man.

"Same time next week in town," Ralph said, surprising him. "There's a small tea shop, opposite the Museum."

"Why the cloak and dagger arrangement?"

"Next week," said Ralph. "Have a solution ready, together with an estimated cost." He turned away and climbed into his old Land Rover and drove off.

Graham stared after him, exasperated. Moodily, he took a few steps over the uneven surface of the track, trying to think of ways to make it more presentable. The cost could be prohibitive, but he had no idea how deep his employer's pockets were. Ah well, he thought, solving problems were how he made a living. He would go home and start making enquiries.

Ralph Cobden might well be eccentric, but so far, he had been easy to work for. He just hoped he had plenty of money in the bank. He wipes the mud from his boots and climbed into his powerful car.

Graham entered the little teashop. Ralph Cobden was sitting in a corner. He was wearing dark glasses and his hood was pulled up over his ears. The effect, thought Graham, was absurdly like a second-rate spy film. He took a seat and opened his briefcase. He produced three plans, duly costed. The most expensive of the three involved a complete rebuilding, either of part of the track as far as the first bend, or over its complete length. It would necessitate the use of a bulldozer. This was also horrendously expensive. The cheapest solution involved spreading ballast, but only as far as the first bend.

It was clear that none of the ideas truly appealed to Ralph Cobden. However, he had been so horrified at the sight of the bright, white surface that he was determined to do something about it. He opted reluctantly for the third option. He took the documents and told Graham he would make a final decision within a week. He would meet him in the same place in a weeks' time with his decision. Then he left.

Graham noted that he had not even been offered a cup of tea. He ordered one for himself and reflected on the curious nature of the man he was dealing with. He resolved to ensure he had a signed agreement before he proceeded with this further contract.

Ralph paid another visit to his bank. This time the manager kept him waiting while he dealt with another client. Ralph waited in the foyer. His curious appearance drew attention rather than affording anonymity. He was no longer in the habit of cleaning his shoes. His coat fell to his knees, and he kept the hood over his head. The bottom part of his face was once more covered by a thick and untidy beard, above which he wore dark glasses. To some he looked sinister, to others comic. Ralph himself had little thought for the impression he made. To assist him in shutting out the world he also wore his earplugs. When the bank manager ushered his previous visitor out and called for "Mr Cobden," Ralph did not at first hear him. He did hear his name the second time and stood up. The manager was nonplussed by his appearance but led the way into his office.

Ralph's statement that he needed a great deal more money to complete the project he was working on was not greeted with great enthusiasm. A loan was out of the question because the cottage was not an asset which the manager considered valuable enough to use as security. It was not even finished. The only way the proposed changes to the road could be financed was by selling some of Ralph's shares. He would not be ruined, but his income would be severely restricted. He was advised not to go ahead. He would not be dissuaded, however. At the end of the conversation, Ralph had his way. The bank manager was not happy. He was not even sure that this strange, young man was entirely sane. However, he helped him make the appropriate arrangements with the broker.

A mixture of coarse sand and ballast was delivered in due course by a large articulated lorry. The material was tipped in large heaps, each of which had to be flattened in turn by a bulldozer. Six complete loans were just enough to cover the surface as far as the first bend. The stark, white chalk was hidden beneath a strangely out of place sandy covering. When Ralph looked at the results, he was far from satisfied, but this was the best that he could do to disguise the dreadful scar. The sand filtered down between the larger grains of chalk and in a comparatively short time even the delivery trucks disturbed the surface. The bulldozer had succeeded in compacting the surface to a degree, but soon the sandy mixed with some of the chalk. Months later, when Ralph was finally settled in the new cottage, he remained very dissatisfied. The only consolation was that the edges of the track over time were populated by greenery of all kinds, thus making it look a little narrower, but it remained unsightly. Initially, it remained a very unpleasant scar and Ralph felt responsible for it. He had certainly not foreseen just how much disturbance his decision to rebuild the cottage there would entail. He had poured a great deal of money into the project. He felt that he was unfairly blaming Graham, but the already cool relationship between the two men became a little more distant. Ralph continued to visit the site once a month until the operation was closed down in February, when the last load of sand and gravel had been delivered, spread like icing to disguise at least partially the worst of the chalk as far as the first bend. From that point to the very top, where the caravan remained perched at the side of the road at the entrance to the quarry, the track remained stark white. He came to hate driving that part of the track. The quarry, now deserted, was also badly affected by all the work. It would be impossible to replace the caravan in the quarry itself. The garden was full of weeds and much of the fence had been badly damaged. And every time he visited the quarry or lurched past it, he saw the great, uneven boulders of chalk which always reminded him of tombstones.

Both Ralph and his project manager were anxious to return to the main business of completing the cottage. For Graham this was a matter of finding tradesmen to work inside the building, including carpenters whose first job would be to fit the windows and doors. But there were still major jobs to be completed outside – the installation of a septic tank, the building and installation of a diesel engine to power the generator, storage tanks and an attempt at landscaping the area immediately around the building. He was secretly pleased that the caravan would no longer fit in the quarry. He agreed to find space for it in the area near the cottage, but it could not be moved before the remaining deliveries had been made. There was simply not enough room within the flattened area for lorries to deliver bulky goods if the caravan were to be parked there. It meant that Ralph was obliged to wait a further six weeks after the work men had returned.

So, the entire project had taken the best part of three years to complete. In all this time Ralph had no settled abode. The nearest he came to it was the period he spent in the caravan. He did not count the time he lived in town. When, at last, the complicated plumbing and electrics were finished, summer was nearing its end. The furniture vans (there were two) that brought his belongings from storage, lurched, and bumped their way up the chalk track. The drivers, not prepared for this, told Ralph in no uncertain terms that this was the worst delivery they had ever made. When, five hours later, they departed, lurching, and slipping on the chalk, Ralph heaved a sigh of relief. The men had at least assembled his bed and his wardrobe was in place, but every room was full of boxes. The floors, fitted with care by the builders, were muddy and dirty. But he was at home.

The fuel for his diesel engine, which was discreetly housed in a separate building nearby, had been delivered by a very small tanker, the driver of which had also complained. Ralph had felt obliged to hunt out his wallet and tip the driver. He had been instructed in how to operate the engine and the electrical pump which brought water from the borehole. The plumbing had been very carefully planned so that freshwater from the pipe was available as a drinking water, but a large storage tank in the loft meant that a hot water system was also installed. He was thus able to take a shower or have a bath. Having to rely on the generator was a difficulty he could not avoid. If he turned off the engine overnight, he would have no electricity and would need to use some other means to find his way round. That was preferable to running the thing night and day, but it meant he would turn the engine off in the evening and find his way back to the cottage and eventually to his bed by the light of a torch. Unfortunately, it also meant that he had no power in the morning until he turned on the engine. That proved to be troublesome on the occasional mornings of deep frost. But these were problems of his own making, and they were part of the price he was prepared to pay. The cottage was an enormous improvement on the caravan.

Single-handedly, unpacking was to take him many weeks. He was desperate to unpack his books and fill up all the beautiful shelves which the builders have provided in his study. However, his first concern was to sort out the kitchen. Next, and much easier, was his bedroom. He had few clothes. The living room was a little more problematic, since it involved major pieces of furniture – a table and chairs, easy chairs, and the sideboard. It was only when he got to the study that many smaller, personal items came to light, including photographs. He had for so long been preoccupied with the caravan and all the building work that he had half-forgotten many of the once very familiar items which had been an intimate part of his life with Gillian. He had spent almost double the time he had shared with Gillian as man and wife, and he had been so busy for most of that time that he had dulled the pain of remembering. Now, as he delved into the carefully wrapped contents of the boxes, he unearthed photograph albums and framed pictures which he had all but forgotten. A large, framed picture of his wife was revealed as he stripped back the paper wrapping, reminding him of delicious moments when they had reverentially each removed the other's clothes. The memory came as an intense shock and all at once his body ached for her. He was forced to sit down and for several minutes he could not move.

There were many, similar moments, most of them less intense, but the unpacking of all these personal belongings, especially those which had belonged to Gillian herself, the contents of her dressing table, brought him pain. He had not expected this. For days on end, he was almost unable to function, and unpacking became an emotional ordeal.

His books on the other hand were solace. They were like old friends. They comforted him, reminding him of imaginary adventures and places he had never visited except in his imagination. He loved the feel of the books, and he dusted them carefully one by one as he arranged them on the shelves. His old desk was placed in front of the window, through which he had a view of the grass, sloping gently upwards towards the top of the Down. The room was piled high with discarded boxes. Several of them were tea chests. All of them were stuffed full of wrapping paper. He had no desire to keep any of this. He took several journeys down to the quarry had made a huge pile, then he set light to it. The paper and wood crackled, and flames leapt high in the air smoke and scraps of burnt paper floated in a tall column which resolved itself ultimately in a pile of ash. He had built this bonfire on his garden quite deliberately, feeding the resultant carbon into the soil. Back indoors he swept and then mopped all the floors until, six weeks after he had first arrived there, he could really say that he had moved in. The windows remained uncurtained: here there was no one to look in on him.

Once a month or so he drove his faithful Land Rover into town. Sometimes it was because the vehicle itself needed attention or an MOT. He also thought it wise to check his post office box, but his main purpose was to stock up with food. He now had a chest freezer which proved to be a godsend. He did not stay in town on these visits and continued to hide behind his hood, dark glasses, and beard. He also used his earplugs, though this proved to be dangerous on occasion, when he did not hear oncoming traffic. He now had everything he needed at home. He began to find, too, that he sometimes had a more than he needed. Memories came back sometimes like ghosts. When he turned off the generator and went to bed in the dark, sometimes he imagined he saw things that moved in the shadows. These ghosts were possibly figments of his imagination, and he wondered whether some of them were caused by animals. He had only glimpsed deer once or twice, smaller creatures like rabbits appeared at twilight, as did some of the predatory birds such as owls. At home, where he had long since given up the practice of wearing earplugs unless he simply could not sleep, he was conscious of the sounds of both animals and birds, the distant barking of a fox, the occasional flapping of wings, the rustling of creatures in the undergrowth. Once or twice, when out walking, he had seen lizards and snakes. At night, once the lights had been turned off, clouds moved across the face of the moon, or, on cloudless nights the stars twinkled in their millions in a dark sky. He did not need to go outside to watch the sky but often, instead of returning directly from the engine shed, he walked on to the top of the Down to experience a kind of wild freedom.

By the time he had completed his move it was halfway through October and the nights were growing shorter. He was determined to establish the routine he had originally planned for himself. That is, he would spend the mornings on physical work and leave the afternoons free for walking or reading, sometimes both. There was still a great deal of work to be done in the quarry garden. The fencing had to be repaired. The weeds which had grown in the soil had to be removed, but there was no point in trying to sow anything until the spring. The caravan had been moved and was now only a few steps from the cottage itself. He set about making sure it was still watertight but decided not to repaint it. Inside he gave it a thorough cleaning and made sure that everything was dry. He was not sure why he did this since he had no intention of using it and he certainly did not intend to invite anyone else to use it. The physical work was good for him. It kept him reasonably fit. He also needed routine. In the afternoons the weather dictated much of what he did. He still enjoyed being out in the rain and now he had a proper bathroom and a supply of hot water, there was no problem about getting clean and dry. If it was thoroughly uncomfortable, wet and cold, or wet and windy, he returned to his study and his friendly books. He turned especially to poetry, especially the Romantic poets that he knew so well. Living

as he did so close to nature, he was beginning to challenge their views. He was more inclined to think that the nature was indeed "red in tooth and claw" rather than a motherly Earth figure. Whenever he visited Druids Wood, which, for all its strangeness, drew him like a magnet, he experienced the same, inexplicable feelings. If the shadows he glimpsed at night were like ghosts, then the darkly mysterious yew grove caused the hair on the back of his neck stand up as soon as he entered the Wood. He did not believe in the supernatural, he told himself sternly, but there was something about this place which drew him to it and filled him with awe.

Journal

I have changed my mind about calling this cottage 'The Hermitage'. In the course of my reading over the past year, I have come across a fascinating figure from the past, Michel de Montaigne. He came from a wealthy family in the countryside near Bordeaux. His father had made a small fortune from trading in herring. This was the period when Humanism was in its infancy. It was the beginning of the Renaissance, a time when intellectuals throughout Europe were daring to question the teachings of the church. Montaigne's father had curious ideas about his son's education and upbringing. For the first three years of his life the boy was brought up in the home of a local peasant to teach him something of the realities of life for the poor. He was then consigned to the tender care of a tutor with whom he learned to communicate in Latin, which became his first language. He went on to have a distinguished career, including several years as a courtier. He was also involved with the 'parliament'. During this period of his life (he was still a comparatively young man) he met and was deeply admiring of a poet, Etienne de la Boetie, also a humanist He married, but little is known about the relationship, except that he had one daughter, the only one to survive infancy. In 1571 Montaigne withdrew from public life and spent the rest of his time as a thinker and writer. His writing was not greatly appreciated at the time, because it took the form of essays which were full of personal anecdotes and tended to wander off the point. (They are also studded with quotations in the original Latin or Greek). In his study of the first floor of a tower in his château, he had the following inscription written on his bookshelves:

'If the Fates permit, he will complete the abode, this sweet, ancestral retreat, and he has consecrated it to his freedom, tranquillity and leisure.'

He died at the age of 59, having suffered from a disease which made him incapable of speech.

Although I do not compare myself directly with Michel de Montaigne, we have enough in common for me to rename this cottage 'The Tower' and I have had the above quotation painted on a wooden plaque which I have screwed to the top shelf of my bookshelves. What I most like and admire about Montaigne, who lived 500 years ago, was his bold decision to think for himself. Like Luther, Erasmus, and others of this period, he challenged the orthodox teachings of the church. This was, after all, a time when alchemy began to give way to chemistry, when religious revelation was challenged by direct observation by courageous 'freethinkers' like Bacon. It was possibly the most exciting as well as the most dangerous period in the development of modern philosophy.

When I decided to withdraw from the world, like Montaigne, it was because I could see so many faults in current ideology. I hopes to discover a similar taste for 'tranquillity', and now that the builders have disappeared, I am beginning to experience something approaching peace. Montaigne says nothing about his personal relationships, neither with his wife, nor with the poet he so admired, so I assume he was not unduly distracted by such intimate memories. In that we differ. Certainly, I can safely assume he had servants to cook his food and wash his linen. They presumably also prepared a fire to keep him warm, but then, Provence is not often cold. The daily chores I undertake are a distraction. Far worse are the occasional excursions I have to make into town. My isolation is far from complete, since I am finding I need to replenish the diesel for my engine far more frequently than I had thought. All these things distract me.

I find the physical activity in my garden truly worthwhile. Not being able to plant very much at this time of the year is an advantage. As well as allowing me plenty of time to plan what crops I want to grow next year, to help with which I have bought useful books, but this has also enabled me to spend time preparing the ground. Having chopped down and pulled up many weeds, I have been able to use them as green compost. I shall be interested to see the results.

On rainy days I often spend the afternoon here at my desk, tapping away on my faithful typewriter. The last time I was in town I bought several spare ribbons. I have a plentiful supply of paper. I am rereading many of my favourite books and a great deal of the poetry, but I am coming at them from an angle I had not expected. It could be called disillusionment. I have far more in common with the poets of the First World War than with the Romantics. I seem to identify more with pain than with a belief in the sublime. I am also more inclined to talk critically about the technical skill of the writer.

On fine days I walk considerable distances, often but not always along the South Downs Way. Very occasionally I meet a walker coming the other way. Perhaps it is my beard and dark glasses that cause it, but such encounters never result in any kind of conversation. Indeed, most frequently strangers do not even speak but hurry past, looking the other way. That suits me. I do not seek out conversations. I have never so far met anyone on my visits to the woods on the southern slopes – not the Druids Wood, which is further to the east. By contrast to the sombre and disturbing eeriness of the yew wood, the mixed timber of this area of the wood is refreshing. There is a considerable mixture. There are a few oaks and elms, inhabited by squirrels that skip and frisk among the branches and watch me with their bright eyes. There are a few evergreens, including holly and small fir trees. At the entrance to the wood there are lots of ash trees and a little further in, the slope begins to increase towards the south, and on this slope, there is a stand of beech trees. At the moment the deciduous trees have all shed their leaves, but I love the sight of the branches which sway and clatter in the wind. Unlike the Druids Wood, possibly because there is plenty of light, these trees are full of life even in the autumn and winter. This is where most of the birds nest. I have still to learn how to recognise the different bird calls. When I came down here in the spring my heart leapt at the site of so many wildflowers, native daffodils, smaller, stockier than the cultivated ones, dog violets, carpets of smiling primroses. At the same time the grass outside the wood was full of cowslips, pretty, tender little plants. Just now the ground on the outskirts of this little would is thick with conkers from two large horse chestnut trees. With all this natural splendour to explore I still do not understand why I find myself so attracted to the gloomy Druids Wood.

When I sit at my desk and think about these things, I recognise that there is something vaguely unhealthy about my thinking. I do not understand why the dark lifeless mass of the yews had such an appeal, nor can I fully understand why the slabs of white chalk at stand round the edge of the quarry remind me every time of the cemetery. I think about death in the countryside. The shrieking of owls reminds me that they are seeking to kill some small creature that rustles in the grass. The sharp bark of a fox and the startled, noisy alarm call of a pheasant bring instantly to mind a picture of death, while once I even witnessed a bird of prey, possibly a sparrowhawk, stoop to capture a small bird in flight. I am no longer under any illusion. The countryside is full of scenes of life and death. Death, however, is in its way fruitful. The dead leaves of all the trees fertilise the soil. Small birds and mammals that fall prey to larger animals enabled nature to keep a balance between the hunters and the hunted. I wonder where I fit in such a scheme. My life to date has been marked by losses. My father died first. In its way his death remains the least satisfactory because I was never able to resolve differences between us. Perhaps, if he had lived a little longer, we might have come to some kind of understanding. My mother's death was cruel. My break with my father had a lot to do with her unhappiness in the last few years of her life. I can see no way I might have changed that. And then, of course, came the cruellest blow of all, Gillian. More than five years have passed, and I believe I am beginning to come to terms with her death, though I don't think I shall never come to terms with the manner of her death. We had such a short time together! And that time was cut short as the tumour took away the person I had loved and still loved, leaving only a body that was wrapped in pain or talking nonsense until the painkillers silenced her.

Once upon a time, before I was able to think freely for myself, habits formed over years suggested that life had a purpose. That idea, like ideas of fairness and justice, is entirely misleading. Life is a hazardous affair. Like the small creatures that scurry through the grass, trying to avoid the beady eyes of larger animals and birds, we are not in full control of our own fate. Nature is not kind. Nor is it cruel. It has evolved so that creatures and plants survive, but some of the predatory species thrive at the expense of others. When Europeans arrived in

Australasia with their pets, they not only killed many of the native species, but they also killed the human beings as well.

I sat on the grass the other day, thinking about such things, and concluded that the human species will soon kill itself off entirely. In its place the species most likely to inherit the earth is insects, notably ants. There must be many millions more insects on the earth then there are human beings. They make fewer demands on it. Perhaps, where once the largest creatures, the dinosaurs ruled, we humans will give way to the Age of the Insects.

Part Three

As weeks became months and winter gave way to spring Chris, busy with his work, thought less and less about Ralph. He wrote another letter which was ignored. He had no other means of tracking his friend down. He was, in any case, busy with his own life and had other friends. However, from time to time he thought about Ralph and, when he did, it was sometimes with a sense of guilt, sometimes with anger. He felt guilty because he suspected that Ralph's state of mind required help. He felt angry because Ralph's stubborn refusal to listen to reason left no opportunity to help him. Above all he was frustrated that he had no idea where his friend was nor how to contact him.

At Easter he drove out to the quarry. He chose not to risk his car on the newly surfaced track which still looked uneven. Instead, he walked from the road. He noted that the new, smoother surface only extended as far as the first bend. After that the chalk stared back at him, lumpy and white.

When he got to the quarry there was no sign of life. Ralph's caravan was parked to one side of the track, leaning uncomfortably. It was clearly not habitable. As for the quarry itself, some of the chalk had been hacked out. A battered and stained flatbed truck stood forlornly in the middle. Large pieces of chalk, presumably too big to handle, were arranged around the walls. The floor of the quarry, which had once been flat and hard, was now churned up. There had been no rain for several weeks and the uneven ground was difficult to walk on.

The cottage was still boarded up and there were no workmen in sight. Ralph was obviously not here. It was a desolate place and Chris turned quickly away, climbed in his car with relief and drove back to town.

One day he was in the hospital café, snatching a quick lunch. It was even busier than usual. A young woman asked if she could share his table. She turned out to be a new consultant psychiatrist and her name was Zoe. "I think my parents deliberately chose the name because it begins with Z," she said.

"Do you like it?"

"I suppose I do," she said.

"Well, I'm Chris, so we're almost an alphabet apart."

Chris had been working in the hospital long enough to help her with local information, such as the quickest route from the apartment block where she lived. After Easter, in response to an appeal to collect funds for a new scanner, some of the staff formed a choir. The intention was to rehearse once a week and put on a concert to raise funds. Both Chris and Zoe volunteered. They became friends and enjoyed an occasional meal together. They shared an interest in the theatre. It was several months before the friendship changed subtly into a romance.

One day Chris was filling routine prescriptions when he came across one for Mrs Dorothy Clarke. The medication was prescribed by an oncologist. Chris counted out the pills with his usual care and a colleague double-checked the number. Chris asked to be told when the patient called to collect them. It was Arthur Clarke. Once again Chris took a few minutes to chat. Dorothy, as the prescription indicated, was ill. She had been diagnosed with breast cancer. Arthur was distressed, but not excessively so. He understood the serious nature of the disease and the treatment, and he was supported by Dorothy's own courage as well as by the understanding and prayers of their friends. Chris was impressed by the faith and acceptance. He was surprised, given the circumstances, when Arthur asked if he had seen anything of Ralph recently.

"He seems to have left the district," he said. "Several of us still worry about him, poor chap. We remember him in our prayers."

Chris was touched and felt another brief pang of guilt. He told Mr Clarke the little he knew.

"Oh dear!" said the older man. "So, he has even pushed you away?"

"Yes. I told him I thought he was – well – mad to go and live like a hermit. I should have kept my opinions to myself."

"Is there nothing to be done?"

"I can't think of anything much."

They parted, Chris having expressed his hope that Mrs Clarke would make a full recovery, though privately he had little hope.

Zoe lifted her glass and said, "Your health!" Chris was a little slow to respond.

"Is anything the matter?" Zoe asked.

"No, sorry!"

"You seem to have something on your mind," she said. "Has something happened?"

"Not really," said Chris. "I'm sorry if I seem distracted. I bumped into somebody today that I hadn't seen for a while."

"Oh? Someone you didn't want to see?"

"No, nothing like that, though the news was not particularly pleasant. An acquaintance of mine – I can't even call them friends more like friends of friends – had some bad news. A lady I know has breast cancer."

"Oh, that's bad luck. Unfortunately, it is pretty common. Still, if it's caught early enough…"

"I suspect it's too late to hold out much hope."

"I'm very sorry. But if the lady in question is only a friend of a friend, as you put it, I'm surprised that it's preying on your mind."

"No, that's not it. It was something that her husband told me, nothing to do with his wife, more to do with a mutual friend."

"All extremely confusing," Zoe commented cheerfully.

"I'm a bit hesitant to tell you about this," Chris said. "You might think I'm trying to pick your professional brains."

"Now you've got me intrigued," said Zoe.

"The person in question is an old friend of mine, or rather, he was an old friend until we had a disagreement. I don't know how else to describe it."

"When people come to me and say, 'I want to tell you about a friend, it's amazing how often they are talking about themselves."

"No, no, it's a friend called Ralph. We met years ago when we were both doing National Service. "

"Oh?"

The waiter came to take their orders. When he had gone, Zoe asked Chris to go on with his story. As he told her about Ralph strange upbringing on the farm and his difficult relationship with his father, Zoe expressed interest.

"What has all that to do with you and your friendship?" she asked.

"I'm not sure, to tell you the truth. All that happened before we met. I had known him for several years when his father was killed."

"Killed? How?"

Chris explained. "I think he always regretted never sorting things out with his father before it was too late," he said. "He was just starting out as a journalist at the time of the accident. He had to give that up to sort out the farm. His mother agreed it made sense to sell up, but it was poor old Ralph who had to do all the work. As I understood it, the big bust up he'd had with his father at the age of eighteen caused problems between his parents and Ralph always felt guilty about that. For all I know he still does."

"It's his mother still alive?"

"No. Once the farm was sold, Ralph helped her move into a small house in town, but she only lived another two years."

"How did he deal with that? To lose both his parents in – what? – two years?"

"Just about two years, yes. He was very fond of his mother, too. At least he had his wife, Gillian."

"Had?' What happened?"

"Gillian died of a brain tumour two years after this."

Zoe looked at him across the table. "That is a terrible story," she said. "I hope he had proper bereavement counselling. I know he had you, but to lose three people in such a short time, at least two of them in the most cruel and bizarre circumstances – well, most people would buckle under the strain."

"What with the sale of the farm and three life insurances, at least he had a lot of money."

"I don't think money will help all that much. Grief is a funny thing."

Chris went on to explain how Ralph had decided to buy a parcel of land in the country and to spend a great deal of money building himself a retreat. He described the new cottage, the quarry, the caravan, and the isolated nature of the spot. He told her of his visits, of the long delays involved in the building and in the changes to the track, and he also told her of his own reaction. Ralph, he said had been completely unreasonable, seeing his disapproval as unwarranted interference. He explained that Ralph appeared to have disappeared, that he was unable to find him or speak to him, that he had written letters to the only address he had, that on the last two occasions he had visited the quarry there was no sign of Ralph. Now he said he felt partly responsible.

The entire meal was dominated by this long, sorry tale. Chris insisted on paying the bill. Previously they had gone Dutch, but he said, apologising, that he had used her professional listening skills. Her part of the bill could be seen as a fee. He walked her home.

"Come in," she said. "I don't want to leave you in this state. I know you've been telling me about your friend, but you were clearly affected by his story. You are part of it, in fact, and while you are obviously concerned for him, I don't think you understand how you have been affected. Come in for another cup of coffee or something stronger."

And Chris did, indeed, find he felt more relaxed than he had for months. Zoe put on some pleasant music, and they sat and sipped their drinks. After a while they stopped talking. It had been a good meal, despite the coffee, alcohol acted as a soporific and Chris closed his eyes. When he opened them again, he found he was reclining in a comfortable chair, covered in a woollen rug. There was no sign of Zoe. He peered at his watch in the dim light – 3.15! He closed his eyes and slept until Zoe woke him with a cup of tea.

"Good morning!" she said briskly. "I hope you're not too stiff. It seemed a shame to disturb you. You were sleeping like someone who was exhausted."

He set up and took a grateful sip of the tea. "I'm so sorry," he began.

"What for? I'm glad you find my chair so comfortable." She was still in her dressing gown and slippers. She sat opposite him on the sofa. It was Sunday morning. Neither of them had work to go to. Zoe prepared a light breakfast and Chris took his leave mid-morning.

Choir practice was on Wednesday, three days later. When it finished, Chris bought Zoe a cup of tea before they left the hospital where they had been rehearsing.

"I've been thinking about your friend, Ralph," Zoe said. "We need to do something about him."

"What?"

"Obviously, whatever is done has to be done tactfully and carefully. It sounds very much as though your friend's reaction to three deaths in rapid succession has taken an extreme form. Grief is very strange and extremely variable. Some people show no signs at all on the surface, others are almost embarrassingly tearful and in anguish. But everybody suffers from grief. Your friend appears to have been trying to hide from it by taking on very demanding tasks, perhaps thinking that all the time he can distract himself with the planning and the execution of the plans, he will have no time to suffer grief. But you say that he has just about finished all the work on his so-called Hermitage. Now is the really dangerous time. And this is the very time when he has chosen to isolate himself."

"But he's out of contact," Chris said. "I don't think it would be very sensible to go blundering in, uninvited. The last time I visited him in his caravan, he certainly did not seem ready to make me welcome. But I am worried. He doesn't answer my letters, assuming he gets them. I haven't seen him for months. The night we had that row in my flat, I could see how he was letting himself go. He was unshaven and grubby. At least, his clothes were. With no one to look after him, who knows what might happen? And one thing which I keep thinking is what would happen if he had an accident."

"Are you happy for me to interfere?"

"In what way? Surely you don't intend to try to talk to him in the cottage, do you? I've told you how he feels about intruders."

"No, don't worry, I think we might be able to come at this from a slightly different angle. It certainly presents a challenge, and it requires patience. I think it best to begin with if you aren't involved. We have to establish contact, that's the first problem. Once that is done and he learns to talk to someone, possibly me, we will be on our way. We don't want to accentuate the breach between you, the aim must be to mend it so that you can be part of the healing process. How does all this sound?"

"It's the most hopeful thing I've heard in months. If you can make it work, I'll be eternally grateful."

"I really mean it when I say it would be better for you not to be directly involved. Can you give me his postal address to begin with?"

Chris did so. He trusted Zoe who had already relieved him of part of his burden of guilt. At least something was going to be done, even if he did not know what.

Zoe's first move was to write a letter on official notepaper. She introduced herself as a newly appointed consultant and said that she was initiating a survey on behalf of the local authority. They needed to know how they could improve their services in a rural area, especially for people living in isolated places. As a first step she was trying to set up a series of interviews. She had noted that he, Mr Cobden, had recently built and moved into a very isolated cottage. Could she possibly use his assistance in identifying the issues involved? She received no reply, so she wrote again. posted the letter to the address which Chris had supplied. After six weeks, pointing out that she had received no answer to her original request, she tried again, emphasising how much help it would give her to learn of the difficulties of living off the beaten track. It would be helpful to her to get his opinion about the various services supplied or not supplied by the council and by the NHS. For example, had he, Mr Cobden, had to take out private insurances because the official provision by the local authority was inadequate? All information would, of course, be totally confidential. She allowed a further month to go by.

Many weeks had elapsed, weeks during which Chris was often tempted to ask if there was any progress in Zoe's attempts to contact Ralph. However, whenever he tried to ask Zoe for information, she told him she had matters in hand and it really was much better for him not to be involved. He was obliged to be content with that, especially since he was beginning to recognise his own feelings for this competent woman were more than those of a platonic friend. They continue to meet at the weekly choir practice, and whenever both of them could find spare time, either in the evening or occasionally at the weekend. The relationship took its natural and inevitable course, and they became lovers. Still Zoe would not tell Chris of her plans to help his friend. Thus, it was that ten weeks after the initial conversation she drove out one afternoon as far as the track to the quarry.

She had dressed in a formal suit. She hesitated, more out of concern for her car than apprehensive about the future interview. The track was already showing signs of wear. Here and there peaks of chalk emerged from the sandy surface. She engaged first gear and began driving up the track. Once past the first bend she found herself driving on an even rougher surface, zigzagging between the larger lumps of chalk. She knew it was no more than half a mile, but it seemed much further when she arrived at last at the entrance to the quarry. She had a large handbag containing a notepad. Remembering the description Chris had given her, she intended to walk as far as the cottage, but inside the quarry itself she saw a man. He appeared to be gardening inside an enclosed space, fenced off with chicken wire. He had obviously heard her coming because he opened a crude gate in this fence, lent his hoe against it, and turned to face her. He did not look welcoming. He was wearing an old, ragged pair of jeans, a stained T-shirt, and a woollen hat. His hair was tied in a ponytail that reached his waist at the back. His face was half hidden in a ragged beard which hung down over his chest as though to counterbalance his hair.

Zoe had approached from the south-west where the afternoon sun was high behind her. She was expecting a hostile reception, so she was startled when Ralph Cobden – it had to be he – was dazzled by the sun. Instead of an angry shout, exhorting her to get off his property, the man at first said nothing but stood stock still.

"Gillian?" he said at last, "Thank God you've come back! You have no idea how much I've missed..." He stopped; the awful realisation struck him down for a moment. Then he shouted, "You're not Gillian! Who the hell are you and what are you doing here? This is private property."

"My name is Sinclair, Dr Sinclair," Zoe replied calmly. "I have written to you. I need your help."

The shock and disappointment made Ralph strangely weak at the knees. He staggered slightly and sat suddenly in a nearby wheelbarrow. He needed time to recover. Zoe watched him but remained where she was. Ralph did not speak for a while. He did not fully understand his own reaction, but he was no longer in control of the situation. This well-dressed woman who looked so like his dead wife watched him while he sat in his undignified wheelbarrow seat. He could feel his heart pounding and a familiar, painful emotion left him gasping for breath.

"Are you all right?" Zoe asked at last. "I'm sorry to have given you such a shock."

"You're not supposed to be here," he said.

"Well, I am here now, and I'm a doctor. Where is your cottage? I think you need a cup of tea."

Ralph glared at her, but she was right, with the sunlight behind her, as this young woman was remarkably like Gillian. The resemblance was still causing him to feel confused. He struggled to his feet and brush the soil from his bottom before leading the way without speaking.

Zoe was agreeably impressed by the cottage, and further surprised when she followed him indoors. It was remarkably clean and tidy. She followed him into the kitchen where he sat at a small table, allowing her to make a pot of tea. She poured a cup for each of them and sat opposite.

"Are you feeling a little better?" she asked.

"Yes. I'm fine now."

"Who is Gillian?"

"Gillian is – was my wife."

"Was, you say. What happened to her?"

"Not that it's any of your business," he replied with a touch of spirit," but she died."

"I'm so sorry. Was it recently?"

"What difference does that make?"

"No, I suppose it doesn't really make a difference, though they do say that it gets easier as time goes by."

"Whoever 'they' are, they're lying."

"So, it wasn't recently?"

"Six years."

"I'm sure she would have loved this place," Zoe said.

"I don't think she would. Something to do with the furnishing, I expect. No curtains, you see."

"Well, since I'm here," Zoe said, taking her notebook from her bag, "maybe I can ask you the questions now."

"What questions?"

"I told you in the letter," she explained. "We are trying to find out in what ways the local authority can help people like you, living in isolated, rural homes."

"I don't want help from the council or from anybody else."

"Right, that's fine, but do you mind if I ask you more specific questions like help with postal deliveries, food supplies, fuel supplies, communications and, most importantly of course, health problems."

"I can look after myself. Do I look starved?"

"No, not at all. How do you get your food delivered?"

"I have a Land Rover. I drive into town to collect stuff like that."

"I see. I also see that you have electricity."

"I have my own generator here. If you listen, you can hear it."

They fell silent and Zoe became aware of the quiet throbbing of an engine somewhere nearby. She got up to look out of the window.

"You won't see it from there," he said. "It's housed in its own, brick- built building, like a small garage."

"Oh! What about fuel? Surely you can't bring that here in your Land Rover?"

Now that she had got him talking, Ralph seemed more than willing to tell her about his cottage and a great deal about his way of life, including his aim is to be self-sufficient, grow his own food.

"Don't you ever get lonely?" Zoe deliberately asked the question artlessly.

"No, I'm not alone."

The answer was intriguing, but this was not the time to pursue it further. Ralph Cobden seemed to be coping remarkably well, but there were one or two areas which Zoe would like to pursue further.

"Thank you very much indeed for all your help," she said, standing up. "I like your cottage and I must congratulate you – or do you have someone to come in and help clean it?"

"I don't welcome visitors," said Ralph, "at least, not usually. You are an exception. Maybe because you are a doctor."

"That is one of the questions I would like to ask you about. I wonder what would happen if you had an accident. I can't see a telephone here."

"I haven't got one and I don't want one."

"Look," said Zoe, "you've been so helpful. Can I come back again to ask just one or two more questions?"

"No."

"In that case, thank you, but you say you come into town to collect your food supplies, could you perhaps to me the favour of calling in to talk to me in my own office? I'll make you some tea of my own and are even supply biscuits."

"I don't like hanging around in town unless it's essential."

"Don't you ever have reason to spend an hour or so in town?"

"Only when I have my MOT or some other repairs." "

"And when is the next time?"

"You are beginning to ask too many questions," he said.

"I tell you what," said Zoe, reaching into her bag, "I have a prepaid, addressed envelope here. It's what I would normally expect you to put your replies in, if you were filling in the form. The next time you're coming into town put the date and time on a piece of paper and posted to me the week before. My name, my job, and my office address, together with a telephone number is on the paper. I'll just add your name, so I know who it's from."

She left the envelope on the kitchen table and walked back to her car.

There were several things which worried her. The most important one was possibly that Ralph Cobden tended to confuse past and present. He was prepared to believe that his wife, who had died six years ago, could be alive. He had also said that he was "not alone" in the cottage. She was not sure what that meant. His insistence that he was able to look after himself was true up to a point: he appeared to be healthy and reasonably fit, and his housekeeping was of a remarkably high standard. She could forgive him for wearing old clothes to do his gardening, though she was not entirely sure about the length of either his hair or his beard. His appearance may not be significant. She would certainly like to talk to him further.

But Ralph had no intention of continuing the conversation. He had been caught off guard and he still felt strangely rattled by her visit. Three weeks after this he made a visit into town, but he did not seek out Dr Sinclair. Her startling resemblance to his dead wife resulted in several confusing moments when a trick of the light or a sudden movement re-awoke similar illusions. Each time he caught his breath with shock and had to sit down for a few minutes. These fleeting apparitions were distressing in themselves, but they led to more strange experiences.

One gloomy afternoon he walked as far as Druids Wood. In the twilight everything looked indistinct. He sat, as he often did, on a thick branch which grew almost horizontally no more than a foot above the ground. He realised he had not removed his earplugs. He had put them in his ears to mask the sound of the generator that morning. Now he took them out and placed them in his pocket. The faint breeze caused the branches above his head to whisper and groan. He had not been aware of these sounds before. They began to resemble human speech, causing the flesh on the back of his arms to creep. He could not distinguish the words. He stood and walked as quickly as he could to the open Down.

That night he sat up late in his study. It was very dark outside. He was trying to make notes from a book. He glanced up for a moment at the window in front of him. His own, dishevelled image stared at him. It was the only thing moving in his sight and he uttered a gasp of surprise and dropped his pen. As he did so, a second face appeared briefly next to his own reflection. It was only momentary, but he believed it to be Gillian.

In the weeks that followed he experienced similar things. He began to be afraid of the dark and went into town to buy ready-made curtains which he nailed to all the windows. He was unable to draw these curtains to let in the light, so he was obliged from that moment to live in darkness or semi-darkness. However, his problems were not over. Once he had turned off the engine for the night – the deep-freeze remained effective until the morning – and he had returned in the darkness to a lamplit kitchen, ashamed of his now familiar fear, he removed his earplugs. Instantly he became aware of the intimate noises of small creatures and the occasional, distant sound of the wind, if the air was not still. Inside, by the light of a torch, he went to bed, usually well after midnight, though he had no way of telling except by checking a clock. He was woken at dawn by birdsong, and it was only when he opened the kitchen door that he knew the sun had risen.

He had grown accustomed to the sound of owls, but now that these strange sensations had begun to pester him, and he had begun to feel fearful, a much more disturbing change was his sensitivity to these calls. He had spent his childhood within earshot of barn owls. Now he would sometimes wake in the night in total darkness and here the eerie sound beyond the window. Like the whispering of the branches in the Druids Wood, the plaintive hooting came to sound like a human voice. He could not make out the words and he strained to do so. He would sit up in the darkness, sometimes dragging the improvised curtain to one side to peer out. He was unable to see any detail, but he often glimpsed movements which he told himself were animals, possibly deer, rabbits, or foxes. He would then let the curtain drop again, shiver and get back into bed. Often, as he did so he had a very strong feeling that there was someone else in the room. He turned on his torch, but the room was always empty.

As time went by, he became more and more convinced that there was someone else in the room, not only at night, but during the evenings. The curtained windows shut him in almost as effectively as solid walls. The imagined voice or voices that he heard became more frequent. He had for some time begun to talk to himself. He found it essential to express his thoughts in words. He did not record in his Journal the exact day that he began conversing with the "voice" which accompanied the strong feeling that he was not on his own. He could only assume it was Gillian. He had never believed in a spirit world before he moved here, but there was definitely something about Druids Wood which was supra-normal. All these sensations of hearing, seeing, feeling, suggested that something was trying to impinge on his consciousness. Gillian, with her strong belief in the supernatural, must be trying to get through to him. At first, he thought this explanation, then he slowly began to take comfort from it. Irrational and unlikely though it was, it could be true. And, if it were true, he needed to make every effort to do his part if the communication was to improve. When these moments occurred in future, he decided he would make a strong effort to calm his fears and allow whatever or whoever it was to speak to him in whatever way was appropriate. From the moment he made this decision he became much calmer. When the owls hooted, he spoke soothing and sometimes loving words to his wife. When he sat up in bed and felt her presence, he relaxed quite deliberately as though he were meditating.

One night he turned off the engine of the generator, lock the door behind him and walked in the darkness towards the kitchen. The battery of his torch failed. He could make out the faint glimmer from the oil lamp he had already lit in the kitchen, it made a faint line down the edge of the door. It was quite dark otherwise. Gingerly, Ralph made his way towards the door. He tripped on a stone, turning his ankle in an unnatural direction, and heard a crack. It was extremely painful. He managed to keep his damaged left leg straight but to roll into a semi--sitting position. He did not put any weight on his left foot. He folded his right leg under him and grabbed the large stone in both hands to push himself upright. He cried out with pain but there was no one to hear him. Slowly and painfully, he hopped. There were no more rocks. He made it to the door and clung to the latch for a moment while his left foot throbbed. He made it inside and sat on a chair, trying to think what to do next. He reflected sourly that other people had asked him what he would do in the event of an accident. He had never answered them. Now he realised the situation was quite serious. His left ankle was very painful. The least move sent excruciating pain up his leg. Fortunately, there was no one to hear him shout.

After thinking for some time, he stood on his good leg and retrieved a broom. It had a sound handle, and he could use it as a crutch. He replaced the batteries in his torch and struggled into a coat. Slowly and carefully, he made his way round the corner of the building to his Land Rover. For a few moments he clung to it, waiting for the worst of the pain to subside, then he made a superhuman effort to scramble into the driving seat. It took a long time and he had to stop several times. He used his hands to lift his left leg to the left, away from the pedals. He was sweating with the effort. He managed to use his right leg on the clutch pedal and to select Four-Wheel Drive, before moving his right foot onto the accelerator pedal. Then he turned the key. To his relief the vehicle did not stall but began to move at a crawl. Hastily he turned on the lights and concentrated on steering. In this way, sometimes screaming with pain, he made his way down the track until he reached the road. He was unable to move his right foot from the accelerator to the brake. He lurched and his foot slipped. He cried out in agony as his ankle sent pain searing up his leg and he lost control.

Four young men, returning from an evening out, found the Land Rover on the wrong side of the road, head down in a small ditch. The lights were on, but the engine was not running. The young man in the passenger seat ran to look inside.

"The driver is inside," he shouted. "He looks in a bad way. I don't think there's much we can do, but I'll stay here. Drive on and find a phone somewhere. An ambulance and the police."

The car drove off at speed into the night. The young man reached inside, but the driver was lying at an awkward angle. He appeared to have struck his head on the windscreen and there was quite a lot of blood which had run down over a large beard. There really was not much he could do on his own, so the young man stared helplessly, pulled his flimsy coat around his shoulders, and stood in the road to wait for help. It seemed to take for ever.

The young man's friends returned several minutes after an ambulance and a police car. A policeman set out warning signs. A paramedic took a preliminary look inside the Land Rover. Ignoring the blood, he felt for a pulse. The driver was still alive. It would be difficult to get him out of the vehicle. Before he could worry too much about that a fire engine arrived. All three services worked closely together. They extricated the driver. They were all disconcerted by his appearance, especially the length of his beard and his hair. They also noticed that he had a stout, broom in the cab which he must have been using as a crutch, judging by the mud on the handle. They looked at his legs and saw that his left foot was twisted at an unnatural angle. He remained unconscious and they got him onto a stretcher and into the ambulance and so to Accident and Emergency in town.

The injuries were severe. The patient had a cracked skull, broken nose and facial lacerations, a broken collarbone, a broken right arm, two broken ribs and a badly dislocated left ankle. He had also lost blood. He was not carrying any form of identification except for a prepaid, addressed envelope. It was addressed to one of the consultants in the hospital inside the envelope was one small slip of paper on which was written Ralph Cobden. A check with the DVLA revealed that the Land Rover was licensed to Ralph Cobden. The address given was a flat in town. When the police attempted to contact the tenants, they explained that they had only moved in three months earlier. So, it was the contents of the stamped, addressed letter that was the only clue to the driver's identity.

Zoe Sinclair was surprised, soon after she arrived for work that morning, to be asked on the telephone by a policeman if she knew someone called Ralph Cobden.

"Yes," she said, "he is a sort of patient of mine."

"Ah! In that case, Dr Sinclair, could you spare half an hour and join us in Resuss? We think your patient may have had an accident last night. We need someone to identify him."

"What kind of accident?"

"A road traffic accident. He appears to have driven himself off the road."

"Oh dear! What injuries?"

"Serious. Several broken bones and a cracked skull, but he's been patched up and they say he'll be okay in time."

"I'll be right down."

Recovery was going to take a long time. The concern centred on the skull fracture. The other broken bones would mend in due course. It was very fortunate that there had been no internal injuries. The ward sister told Zoe as much as she could. The patient was still unconscious. He was being monitored and the nurses were watching and waiting for him to regain consciousness. It would, they knew, be a critical moment. Had there been any injury to the brain? They waited three days. On the third day the patient opened his eyes briefly. The eyelids fluttered. He did not speak but relapsed into sleep almost immediately. He woke again two hours later. This time, when the nurse spoke to him, he tried to speak but produced only an incoherent sound. The nurse asked if he wanted water. With an effort he replied yes, and the nurse gave him a drink through a straw. He swallowed. He was not able to change his position. He opened his eyes wide, saw only the face of the nurse and a piece of the ceiling. His ribs hurt when he breathed, and they hurt even more if he made an attempt to move in the cot. He closed his eyes again, tried to sleep to escape the pain which seemed to be in all parts of his body.

Zoe told Chris of the accident, but she advised him not to visit his friend before she had chance to speak to him. She wanted to assess the damage, but it was complicated by the concern she already had about his state of mind and before the accident occurred. The physical injuries were themselves serious, she said. For the immediate future it would be best to allow Ralph to adjust. She would try to inform him gently of his situation. For the moment it would be wise not to awaken too many memories. Chris listened and accepted her advice reluctantly. Zoe suggested that he might drive out to the cottage to check that all was well there so, two days after the accident, he drove to Deadman's Down.

It was several months since he had been there. He was not sure what to expect. The police had already visited the cottage to make it secure, but Chris obtained the keys with Zoe's help. He noted that the caravan was parked close to the house, and he looked inside. All was in order, but he left the door open while he visited the cottage to air the van. He remembered how damp it had been inside the last time. He walked to the kitchen door and let himself in. At 10 o'clock in the morning it was very dark inside and he was surprised and disturbed to see that Ralph had attached curtains to the window frame by nailing them. Ralph was good with his hands. He had a range of tools, including power tools, and he had always taken pride in his own workmanship. It was completely out of character for him to resort to using nails in this way. Chris found a toolbox in a corner of the kitchen. It contained pliers and pincers. He removed the nails and folded the curtains as the light filled the kitchen once more. He went from room to room, increasingly worried to find curtains nailed up in this way at every window. He took them all down, folder them neatly and place them on the bed. Then methodically he checked all the windows and doors. He had already discovered that the electric lights did not work, but he remembered that the power came from a generator outside the cottage itself.

On the back of the kitchen door was a hook from which hung a small collection of keys. Armed with these he made his way to the building a short distance away and let himself in. He was not familiar with the machinery, but it was well looked after. There seem to be two elements, an engine, recognisable in part by an exhaust pipe which led through the wall and by a driveshaft that led to a metal case on which this there were several gauges. On all of them the needle pointed to zero. There was also a large, red switch which was in the Off position. Chris thought it wise to leave all this well alone. He locked the door and returned to the cottage. The kitchen smelled faintly of paraffin and on the table, there was a paraffin lamp. He picked it up and shook it gently. It appeared to be empty. He un-screwed the lid of the container. It was indeed empty, but he noticed that the wick had not been turned down to extinguish the lamp. He deduced that it must have burnt itself out. There was nothing more he could usefully do. He locked up and returned to his car. The track, though negotiable, was still quite rough. Before he drove away, he looked inside the quarry. It was a sad sight. Ralph's "garden" was already populated by weeds inside the protective wire. The floor of the quarry itself was very badly churned up by heavy vehicles and the chalk face was no longer undisturbed: a substantial amount of chalk and material had been hacked out, leaving a very uneven surface. On two sides of the quarry walls several very large chunks of chalk had been roughly arranged, restricting any room there might have been. It was instantly obvious why the caravan had been moved. Chris looked at it and thought sadly that Ralph's efforts to make a home for himself in a beautiful spot had resulted in further desecration. The quarry was now a hideous scar. The cottage was attractive in a rustic way, but the area around it was still unnaturally flat, exposed chalk, soil, and builders' rubble. Perhaps, given time, nature would reclaim some of the damaged area, but for the moment it was simply ugly.

He drove away down the bumpy track thinking how badly Ralph's plans had gone awry. One of the worst aspects was that other people had warned of the dangers. He had been told that the plan was financial disaster, yet he had insisted on going through with it. He had rejected friendships, including that of Chris himself. He had been warned of the danger that would follow if he had an accident, though that has not included a road accident. (Later, when all the circumstances were revealed, Chris was to learn that the entire calamity, including the crash, had been caused by a broken ankle.) So, the journey back to town was a time for regret and frustration.

He was fortunate to have found Zoe Sinclair. She was practical as well as sympathetic. Ralph was badly injured, but Zoe had insisted that it would be unwise of Chris to visit him yet. As well as several broken bones, she told him, he had suffered some serious head injuries which were giving concern to her and to the resident neurologist. Ralph had not yet fully regained consciousness. He had opened his eyes a few times but had been unable to respond to questions. The consultants were especially concerned with the head injuries. The skull had been fractured, causing swelling to the brain. They could do little but wait. The patient, meanwhile, was receiving close monitoring and kept in a quiet environment. Chris would be shocked when he saw him next, according to

Zoe. In order to clean up for the operations they had been obliged to shave his head and his beard, removing quantities of hair, and exposing the skin which was starkly white. When Chris was eventually allowed to visit his friend, he was indeed shocked.

Three weeks passed. Ralph began to show signs of recovering. He spoke to the nurses and to the doctor to ask for water and to ask how he had come to be in a hospital bed. It was quite obvious why he was there. His broken leg was in a cast, he was strapped, unable to move one arm, which nevertheless caused pain from time to time, he had bandages around his head and breathing was painful. He had no recollection of the accident. Indeed, he seemed confused about his past. He asked questions but he had little ability to concentrate, so the questions tended to be unconnected. He learnt very slowly that he had been in a road accident. He learned there was no one else involved. He asked where it had happened but appeared not to understand the reply. Deadman's Down he recognised but looked puzzled, not knowing why he should be there. Several times he asked about his mother, why had she not visited. The confusion, which Zoe reported faithfully, was not uncommon in cases like these. Ralph appeared to be suffering from retrograde amnesia, a condition which seemed very alarming to the onlookers as well as the patient, but one which would probably resolve itself. The neurologist was particularly concerned with the swelling on the brain, but that, too, slowly healed. The physical damage was considerable. Confined to a bed for weeks on end, Ralph began to lose his normal fitness. He also lost weight. When at last the physiotherapists helped him to stand up, he almost had to learn how to walk again – not easy, since his broken leg made it difficult.

By this time Chris was a regular visitor. Patients with this kind of amnesia, Zoe told him, were helped by emotional support. He was disconcerted to begin with when Ralph did not recognise him, and he was forced to explain they have known one another for years. He explained how they had shared National Service and University. Ralph was politely interested. The amnesia meant that Ralph had forgotten a huge section of his past. Bit by bit Chris began to fill in the gap. As he did so,

Ralph's memories slowly returned, but it was not dramatic nor spectacularly clear. Chris was hesitant to stir up too many distressing memories, so it was with trepidation one day that she mentioned Gillian. He watched his friend's face. Ralph frowned in concentration then, as the name triggered first an image, then a growing realisation that Gillian had been an essential part of his life, a happy smile lit up his features briefly. Then the fuller memory turn joy to grief.

"She's dead, isn't she?" he asked.

"It was six years ago," Chris said.

"Six years! What has happened since?"

"You decided to build yourself a cottage on Deadman's Down."

"And that's where I had the accident?"

"Yes. You drove your Land Rover off the road. No one knows what you were doing."

Ralph said nothing for a while, trying to remember. "I remember!" he said triumphantly. "I broke my ankle."

"I'm afraid you broke more than your ankle."

"No, I mean I broke my ankle at the cottage. That's why I was trying to drive to town. I was trying to use my one good leg on the clutch."

Chris looked at him in astonishment. "You mean you drove down to the main road with a broken ankle?"

"Yes, I had to. It was the only way I can get here. I remember now, I used to broom as a crutch."

Piece by piece he was working out the events of that evening. But it was a big effort. He closed his eyes and Chris left him to sleep.

As his bruised brain slowly resumed its normal shape and his fractured skull began to mend, the neurologist/neurosurgeon handed over his part in proceedings to Zoe Sinclair, who would now deal with the psychological return to normality. Since Ralph had a number of physical injuries to deal with, he was kept very busy by visits from the orthopaedic surgeon and from a succession of physiotherapists. It felt to him that he was constantly undertaking physical exercises of all kinds, most of them painful, but he was slowly regaining muscle strength. Learning how to walk again was a particular effort, but he was determined to succeed. He could not have explained what drove him. He spent little time thinking about the future. He was constantly told by Zoe that his memory would come back in due course, and he should not distress himself by trying too hard. And most of the time he was kept so busy that he lived almost entirely in the present. In this way he was making steady progress without much sign of any real stress.

There were occasional instances of thoughts and even sensations returning unexpectedly. One such instance occurred in his sleep. He had had a more tiring session with the physio in the morning so, after a little lunch, he fell asleep. He woke up in a sweat, his heart beating faster than normal, with a feeling he could only describe as dread.

"Do you remember what you were dreaming about?" Zoe asked.

"It's all a jumble," he said. "I think I was in a forest somewhere, but I was being chased."

"Hunted?"

"I don't know. I have a funny feeling it wasn't people."

"Animals?"

"No, I don't know. They were, well, they felt like ghosts."

"Ghosts?" Zoe found this interesting, but she asks no further questions for the moment.

Ralph felt nervous when the lights were being lowered or turned off later in the evening. He asked the nurse to leave one light on. He felt slightly uncomfortable, ashamed to be afraid of the dark like a small child. By this time, he had been moved from the sideward to one which he shared with seven other patients. As he lay there in the semi-darkness, he was more aware than usual of the sounds. One of the men snored gently. That seemed strangely comforting. Another was attached to a monitor which committed an electronic noise from time to time. Nurses entered the ward, making little noise except when they spoke in hushed tones to a patient. Outside, at the nurses' service station they held quiet conversations during the small hours. All these small noises, together with lights filtering into the ward, made it hard for Ralph to get back to sleep. Sleeping during the day made it very difficult for him to sleep at night.

"Well," said Zoe Sinclair one morning, "your physios are happy with your progress. Provided you don't do anything silly, they think it's time we discharged you. I shall want to keep an eye on you. Ideally, I'd like you to come to see me once a week, but I'm pretty happy with your progress too. I don't think it's a good idea for you to go back to the cottage yet. I think Chris would be quite happy for you to stay in the spare room. How would you feel about that?"

"It would be okay, I think."

"Good. In that case we can discharged you this afternoon. Chris will pack up early and help you move in."

Ralph was not aware that his doctor and his friend lived together much of the time. For the immediate present Chris would return to sleeping in his own flat. He left the pharmacy in the hands of his assistant at 4 o'clock that afternoon. Ralph still used walking sticks and his friend watched anxiously as he made his unsteady way to the car. The short drive was like travelling through a foreign country after weeks spent in the hospital. Fortunately, there were no stairs to negotiate but even so Ralph was relieved to sit down while Chris made them a cup of tea.

"What are you going to do about the cottage?" Chris asked. "It's fairly safe, I suppose. It's so far off the beaten track about the chances of anyone wanting to burgle it are probably remote, but I think you need to keep an eye on it. It wouldn't be very sensible to move back in yet, not if you are having to visit the hospital every week. Do the physios want to see you as well,"

"Only once a month," Ralph said.

"Maybe the best bet would be for me to run you out to the cottage say, once a week, just to check. We have no idea how soon you will be fit enough to move back in, do we?"

Ralph frowned into his cup. "To tell you the truth," he said, "the way I feel at the moment, I don't want to go back at all."

This came as a total surprise to Chris. He remembered the determination with which

Ralph had insisted three short years ago on purchasing the derelict property. He had thrown huge quantities of money on the project. If he did not move back in, what on earth would he do with it? Could you afford to find somewhere else to live? The situation was worse in many ways now that the cottage was built. It would be a few weeks yet before Ralph's ankle would be safe for him to drive with. His Land Rover was written off and he would presumably need to buy a replacement car. While it would be advisable for him not to return to such an isolated place, he had, indeed, ended up with a white elephant. He would never be able to sell it. Chris did not know the state of his friend's finances. Furthermore, although Ralph was more than welcome to use his spare room, it could not be a permanent arrangement. All for the moment the matter was dropped.

Chris was busy every day at work. For a day or two Ralph remained in the flat, but he had been instructed by the physio to exercise regularly. He no longer had his beard to hide behind. That had been shaved together with most of the hair on his head. He wore a woollen hat and, since he still found the noise and bustle in the street difficult to cope with, he used earphones as well as the glasses when he went out. He did not, however, fear being recognised. He had changed. Shaving off his beard exposed very white skin, and several weeks of inactivity resulted in the loss of a great deal of weight, so even his face looked thinner.

He resumed the habit of visiting the library every day. He now enrolled the assistance of the librarian, a kind, intelligent young woman. He told her he wanted to find as much information as possible about Deadman's Down. The deeds on the property gave him little information, except the name of the farmer who had owned the land. The librarian put him in touch with a local historian, a man called Bernard Carter. Formerly a teacher, Bernard had researched the history of Deadman's Down. During the late 18th and early 19th centuries a local man had built the original cottage for a permanent home for the man in charge of the chalk pit and lime kilns. The lime was largely used to make mortar for the flint buildings in the villages nearby. There was a story which Bernard had researched further by reading through reports in local newspapers in the 1800s. It told of the inhabitant of the cottage who, like the lighthouse keepers of the period, had been driven mad by the isolation. A gruesome report told how the man had disappeared and his body had been found several days later in Druids Wood, where he had hanged himself. The chalk pit had been abandoned and the cottage boarded up. It was reputed to be haunted.

Ralph said nothing of this to Chris nor to Zoe. He was by habit a rational man. His experiences of living in the new cottage, however, forced him to regard the story differently. His natural scepticism was challenged by his memories. So, when Chris suggested a quick visit to the cottage one weekend, he made a lame excuse. Chris said that he understood that it might be a difficult experience for him, and suggested that he should go on his own, leaving Ralph behind. Ralph agreed, but Chris sensed there was more to the refusal than the excuse offered.

All was still in order, but Chris remained concerned that the property, despite its remoteness, remained vulnerable, especially since it now contained many of Ralph's personal possessions. The potential burglar was free to peer through the uncurtained windows. He pointed this out to a friend, suggesting that shutters or at least properly hung curtains should be set up. Ralph agreed it was a good idea, but he agreed as though he had little interest.

"Have you any idea when you might want to move back in?" Chris asked.

"I haven't really given it much thought," Ralph said. "I imagine you want to get rid of me. I'll start looking for somewhere else."

"No, no, that's not what I meant at all. You are welcome to stay here as long as you like – permanently if you need to. It's just that I thought you would be worried about your possessions, perhaps even feeling a little homesick for the old cottage."

Ralph shot him a surprised glance. "Homesick? You think I'm missing the place? You couldn't be further from the truth. I honestly don't want to go back there at all."

"Oh!"

"Don't you want to say, 'I told you so'?"

"No. I'm very surprised though. Everybody advised you not to go ahead with the cottage. You were absolutely obstinate. It must have cost you a great deal of money. Why have you changed your mind?"

"I don't think you'd believe me, if I told you. Put it down to the bang on the head. All I know is that I hate the very suggestion of visiting the place, let alone living there again. It was a big mistake, but I'd rather not talk about it, if you don't mind. If you can find a builder willing to take it on, get the place boarded up again. I suppose it would be a good idea to put some kind of large padlock on the doors to the generator too. Just don't ask me to go with you."

Chris let the matter drop, but he reported the conversation to Zoe. He set about finding someone to secure the property. He found a local builder, a man who employed only one worker.

"Deadman's Down? That's at the back of beyond!" the builder said.

"Yes," Chris agreed. "It is. That makes it harder to keep an eye on things," he added. "Do you think you could make it secure?"

"I can board the place up, but I'm not sure that would make it really secure. Anybody wanting to break in could still do so. I can board up the windows and doors, that sort of thing, but that won't stop anybody really determined. A hammer and chisel or a crowbar and anyone could break in."

"Well, will you have a look?"

"Okay, it'll mean at least two trips to measure up and then to take the stuff back in my van."

"That's fine. As soon as you've had a look, give me an estimate and I'll pay up.

"I don't usually ask for payment before the job is complete."

"Whatever you say."

Chris was shocked by the estimate. He told Ralph, expecting at least a surprised reaction but the information was received with indifference.

In fact, although Ralph had insisted on paying his friend for the use of his spare bedroom on a generous scale, as expenditure was otherwise low. He helps with the cost of food, but he seldom left the flat except to visit the library. It never occurred to him to go out in search of entertainment. This might have caused inconvenience and annoyance to Chris, had he not already been in the habit of spending two or three nights at Zoe's flat. It was an arrangement which suited all three individuals for the time being. Both Zoe and Chris led busy professional lives. Both of them were concerned by Ralph's recovery, both physical and mental. The living arrangements presented few problems.

Ralph's broken bones mended. Following doctors' orders, he walked every morning to the nearby park. A path led all the way around the circumference, and he set himself a target which he increased every two weeks. He met few people and seldom paused. He no longer hid his face and, behind the trees which lined the park, traffic and noise was not a problem for him. He grew less anxious. His visits to the library no longer required an act of will. Instead, he actually enjoyed them. Bernard Carter provided interesting information and provoked much thought. Ralph was able to think about the strange history of Deadman's Down without being unduly disturbed now that he did not live there. However, the very thought of returning, even for a short visit, caused him anxiety.

"I think," Zoe said, "I do not need to see you on a regular basis any longer. Physically you are much better, and I believe that your mental health has also improved. What I would like to do is to give you a series of tests. They are generally quite standard. If I'm right, they will show that you are fit for me to release you."

The tests, she explained, would take two hours. They should reveal if the concussion had any long-term effects on cognition. Separate tests would also indicate emotional stability and resilience. Ralph was surprised to find the prospect of losing these regular sessions with Zoe Sinclair was surprisingly worrying. He had grown used to the comfort he felt at having someone who listened without making judgement. It was with mixed feelings that he turned up for the morning of tests. For half an hour he was faced with a series of tests which he found quite familiar. They tested his memory, his use of words and vocabulary, his reasoning ability both with words and with numbers, and his perception of shapes. It was a long time since he had done this kind of intelligence test and he was pleasantly surprised. One or two questions he was unable to answer, but, once he had finished, Zoe told him that his score was much higher than average. There was she said nothing wrong with his cognition. They had a short break with a cup of tea. The second part of his assessment related to his emotions. He was asked to agree or disagree with a series of statements, some of them clearly outrageous, some political, some philosophical. He was then presented with a series of scenarios and asked how he would react to them. It was at this point that he hesitated for the first time. Zoe made notes.

"How did I do?" Ralph asked.

"On the whole very well. However, there were just a few things which left me puzzled."

"Well, some of those questions, the ethical ones and those to do with beliefs, I found very difficult."

"I take it, from what you have told me before, that you have no religious faith?"

"No."

"But you seem to be hesitant, answering questions to do with the supernatural."

"Yes. Look, Doctor, do you believe in ghosts?"

"Ghosts? I'm not sure how to answer that."

"Then you may be able to understand my problem."

"Not really. What exactly is the problem?"

"When I went to live at Deadman's Down, I didn't believe in ghosts, but I'm sure an expert in the paranormal would say the place is haunted."

"What makes you say that?"

"A number of things, experiences I can't explain. I know it's a lonely place – that's why I chose it – and no one lives anywhere near, but I often felt there was someone watching me."

"Are you talking about the new cottage?"

"Not just the cottage. I know there were animals – deer, for example – and other creatures, but I could have sworn there was someone in the house. I began to think that it was Gillian sometimes. There is one place nearby, Druids Wood, which is especially spooky. Apparently, the last man to live in the cottage hanged himself there. It's very gloomy, the trees are all yew trees. If you go into the wood, it's absolutely silent, but I was sure there was someone there. It got so I had to hang curtains at the windows to stop anyone from watching from outside."

"I can see this was very unsettling," she said, "but I'm a rational thinker. I believe there has to be a rational explanation, but that doesn't prevent these experiences being real to you. I can understand why you are reluctant to go back."

"I can't face it," Ralph admitted.

"I assume you have a lot of money tied up in the cottage?"

"Yes," Ralph admitted ruefully.

"Well, I didn't suppose all is OK all the time. Chris is happy to have you stay."

"He has been a true friend, but I'd like a move out some time. I just can't face returning to the Tower."

"Why The Tower?"

Ralph explained.

"But all your belongings are there, I presume?"

"Most of them, yes."

"Well," Zoe said briskly. "Except for the unusual experiences that you describe as haunting, I can give you a clean bill of health. I advise you to steer clear of Deadman's Down, but what you do about your cottage, I don't know. I imagine it won't be easy to sell it."

"No. I imagine not."

At least, Ralph thought, as he walked back into town, his mind was in good fettle and his body was reasonably fit. He could be grateful for that.

Two events were to change the course of his life, one predictable, the other quite unexpected.

Chris came home from the pharmacy in a sombre mood.

"Bad news," he said, "Dorothy Clarke died today."

Ralph was shocked. He knew Dorothy had been ill, but his relationship with her and Arthur had been a rather casual friendship. This new loss, nevertheless, caused fresh grief and fresh guilt, regret that he had not thought to visit the Clarkes for months. With Chris' help, he attended the funeral service. The chapel was full. The Clarkes were well liked. One or two gave Ralph a curious look, some half-recognising him He muttered a few, conventional phrases of condolence as he shook Arthur's hand. A week later he retrieved his old bike and pedalled to the farm. He remembered the dreadful shock of Gillian's death and thought he might ease his friend's pain just a little by offering him a friendly ear. It did not work out like that. He found Arthur in the milking parlour, still cleaning up all the equipment from the morning milking. Ralph had all but forgotten how noisy these places were. Everything was made of shiny, stainless steel which banged and clattered and echoed in the now empty, concrete building, noises which were amplified by the sheer size of the space.

Arthur looked up and saw him. "Hello, young Ralph," he said, without stopping. "What are you doing here? I'm sorry, but I haven't got time to stop today, Charlie, that's my head cowman this has called in sick. He's my right-hand man, so I'm now single-handed for the day and I'm already behind."

"In that case, can I give you a hand?"

Arthur looked at the younger man and smiled. "You're not exactly dressed for the job," he said, "but thanks for the offer."

"Have you got a spare pair of overalls and some rubber boots?"

Arthur straightened up. "You serious?"

"I spent about fifteen years on the farm next door," Ralph pointed out. "I can still remember quite a lot. I might even enjoy it, you never know, and you could have a free farm labourer for the day."

Arthur paused for only a moment. "What size feet?" he asked.

"Tens."

"There's a boiler suit hanging out inside the porch of the house and there's a spare pair of boots underneath. Are you sure you don't mind?"

"I've got nothing better to do."

"If you mean it, I got 15 calves in the barn. I've fed them, but they really need mucking out. There's half a dozen straw bales there when that's done."

To his surprise Ralph enjoyed the work. Arthur clearly appreciated the help since he did not need to explain. There was plenty of work to do. Much of it involved moving livestock, but there was some heavy work, collecting, and carrying sacks of supplementary feedstuffs. Arthur worked hard and efficiently. He asked Ralph to clean out the henhouse, collect the eggs and scatter grain for the chickens. There was no time for chat, but Arthur came to find him at about midday.

"Take a break, boy," he said, "come back to the kitchen. I think you've earned a cup of tea. There's even a piece of cake, sadly it's one I baked. Nobody could bake a cake like Dorothy."

The words were spoken in a surprisingly cheerful voice. Arthur remembered his wife with great fondness but, it appeared, without the heart wrenching grief that had characterised Ralph's own loss several years previously. The farmer made a pot of tea and produced a loaf of bread, butter, cheese and ham and a jar of home-made pickle. The cake was "for afters" he explained. He thanked Ralph again for helping out.

"The trouble these days," he said, "is that you cut down on labour and relying to some extent on mechanisation. Even the cows almost milk themselves these days. It's a long way off milking by hand."

"I remember that," said Ralph.

"Yes, you've done well today."

"How long is Charlie off for?"

Arthur shrugged. "According to his wife, a could be about three weeks."

"So, what are you going to do?"

"I'll have to try to find somebody."

"Look, you and your wife were always very kind to me. What if I came and helped out until Charlie gets back?"

Arthur looked at him in surprise. "I couldn't ask you to do that," he said.

"I've got nothing better to do. I've recovered from all my injuries. I've been trying to get fit by running every day. Working here would be better exercise. I quite enjoyed it this morning."

And so, a deal was struck.

Although Charlie returned to work after three weeks, he was still not fully recovered, and Ralph continued to lend a hand for a further two weeks. He refused to accept payment, saying that Arthur had already paid him a great deal of money for the cattle he had bought from the Cobden Farm.

Farm work is often very solitary business. Even when there were three men, for much of the time they were working on their own. It was only during lunch breaks that there was time for conversation. At the end of the day Charlie got on his pushbike and rode the short distance to his cottage. Often, however, Arthur asked Ralph to "have a bite to eat" before he too went home. Often the food consisted of a hot stew which had been cooking all day in a slow cooker. Arthur was an accomplished cook, something he said he had learned from his wife about whom he talked readily and happily.

"Forgive me saying this," Ralph said one day, "but you clearly loved your wife dearly and you seem remarkably cheerful. How do you manage it? Don't you feel miserable without her?"

Arthur looked at him squarely and soberly. "Of course, I miss her," he said. "I miss her every minute of every day. But I have my faith and despair is not part of it. That's what it's all about."

Ralph did not reply.

"There is one bit from the bible, Ecclesiastes," Arthur continued. "I probably only partly understand it, but I have known it all my life and lived by it, it goes something like this,' To everything there is a season and a time to every purpose under heaven.' It goes on something like 'a time to be born and time to die, a time to plant and the time to pluck that which was planted'. As a farmer I have got to know the seasons. It all makes sense to me. And when it talks about there is a season to be born and a season to die, that makes a lot of sense".

Ralph said nothing for a while, but he felt deeply moved. Later, when he had left and was back in his bed, the conversation repeated itself in his head over and over. There was something admirable about the way the old farmer accepted the life on the terms offered. He was doubtless sustained in part by his belief in life after death, an idea which ran counter to all Ralph's understanding. There was, however, great strength to be drawn from the acceptance of life and death on these terms.

One morning a little later, on his way to the library, Ralph saw a large, red van on the road and, for the first time since before his accident, he remembered he had not visited the post office to check his mailbox. He went straight there. There were half a dozen letters including two that were clearly from his bank. Once he was seated at his customary table, he opened them. As he expected, they contained statements of his accounts. He did not bother to read through but folded them back and returned them to their envelopes. The most recent statement was accompanied by a letter.

"Dear Mr Cobden,

I am a little concerned that you may not be receiving your correspondence. I have no other way of contacting you. If you do receive this, I should be obliged if you would come and see me at your earliest convenience or at least reply. You should have received a full statement a month ago. (The letter was dated three weeks earlier.) I was surprised that you did not contact me at that time. I assume you now have that statement, which includes an extremely important update concerning your dividends and the substantial increase in the value of the stock you hold. There is no cause for alarm or concern if you decide to take no action, but, as you will appreciate when you look at the figures, it might be wise to give some thought to possible changes.

In the circumstances I should be grateful if you could call at your earliest convenience.

Yours sincerely,

(manager)"

Ralph was puzzled by this. He retrieved the statement, now seven weeks old, and looked at the sum deposited under the heading 'Dividend.' He was surprised: the amount was approximately four times what he expected. He had not bothered to keep track of his investments, leaving that to his accountant and his broker. He was not in the habit of reading a newspaper, nor did he attempt to keep up to date with news of any sort, financial or otherwise. He decided to call into the bank. Once more the cashier asked him to wait while she checked. She returned, apologised, said that the manager had appointments all day but would make himself free the following morning at 10 am. Ralph returned to the library. He was curious but the letter had stated there was no cause for anxiety and, looking at the bottom line of each of his three accounts, he was agreeably surprised. He was vaguely aware of having spent large sums of money before the accident many months previously. It had crossed his mind that he should see about replacing his Land Rover but until he had been given a clean bill of health, he was content to walk everywhere in town. He did not want to return to the cottage even for a brief visit, but he knew that he would have to, sooner or later. Chris had generously told him that he was welcome to stay as long as he wished, but the best part of a year had passed. What's more, his reading and research into the history and prehistory of Deadman's Down had caused him to consider some new plans.

His meeting the following morning with Mr Grosvenor, the bank manager, provided yet another shock, a pleasant one on this occasion.

"Do I take it that you have been following the fortunes of Marshall Electronics?"

"No," Ralph admitted. "I have been far too busy recovering from my accident. I don't take much interest in all this as I imagine you realise. I know the company in question is one of my investments. I just signed the documents. I leave the rest to Gordon Scrimshaw."

Mr Grosvenor found this very difficult to comprehend. How could someone invest a sizeable sum and take no interest? He said nothing, however, except to ask if Ralph had not heard the news about Marshall Electronics.

"I'm afraid not," said Ralph a little testily. "I was in hospital for nearly six months, you know."

"I am so sorry. I had no idea. What happened?"

"A road accident," said Ralph. "I broke several bones and cracked my skull."

"I had absolutely no idea," said the manager. "And how are you now? You look different."

"All that facial hair, you mean? Yes, and I have lost several stones in weight. I'm still having counselling from a psychologist."

"In that case," said Mr Grosvenor, "I can well understand why you didn't answer my letters. But the news is good news. Marshall Electronics proved to be a very shrewd investment on your behalf. They were only a small outfit, but their research and development were second to none. Don't ask me to try to explain it – it's all beyond me – but apparently, they have come up with some gadget or other which is going to be very important for military applications. They negotiated a very lucrative deal with the government and their share value went up by a factor of five. You may have noticed you have already received a very large share dividend. "

"Ah, that is good news!"

"Now, you need to make a decision. I'm told that the shares have probably peaked. You can, of course, keep them in your portfolio, but you could decide to sell while they are at their peak and reinvest the money."

"Does it make any difference?"

"Not a great deal, but I don't think your dividends will be quite as high next time".

"If I were to sell," Ralph said thoughtfully, "how much would they realise?"

"Properly managed, because you don't want to sell them all in one lump – that would cause their value to drop – you're holding is probably worth just over a hundred thousand."

Ralph whistled. "I need to talk about this," he said.

"That's precisely why I asked you to come and talk to me."

"There is somebody else," Ralph said, "and I'm not talking about Gordon Scrimshaw."

"I shouldn't leave the decision too long. Markets are always very volatile. The value could drop considerably in a very short time."

"I'll let you know tomorrow."

Ralph did not return to the library but went back to the flat where he looked over the bank statements and the reports from Gordon Scrimshaw, making notes. Then he made a number of telephone calls.

"Hello!" Chris came into the kitchen with a handful of letters. "As a great, thick envelope for you. An Irish stamp! I didn't know you knew someone in Ireland."

"Ah, I've been expecting that. "

"Come to think of it, Ralph, I don't remember your ever receiving letters here."

"No, I've been using a post office box. I hope you don't mind."

"Mind? Why should I mine? You live here, after all."

"Good. I've given up the post office box."

So, thought Chris, he's not going to tell me what's going on. No more was said, although the first letter with the Irish stamp was followed by three more. Chris noticed that each carried the logo of Trinity College, Dublin. He assumed that Ralph was doing some sort of research.

Several more weeks passed until one evening Ralph asked, "Are you and Zoe going to be free next Saturday evening?"

"I think so," said Chris. He checked his diary. "Yes, I'm free and I think Zoe is, too. Why?"

"I want to take you out for a meal somewhere. Nowhere too posh. I thought the Cricketers Arms. It supposed to be quite a good gastropub."

"Sounds good," said Chris. "What's the occasion?"

"Tell you on Saturday," said his friend and would say no more.

The Cricketers Arms was a pleasant, old-fashioned pub, cosy, low-ceilinged. It was becoming fashionable. Ralph and Chris arrived by taxi "so we can enjoy a glass of wine, Ralph pointed out. A young girl took them to their seats where they were joined by Zoe. They had scarcely ordered their drinks when Mr Clarke arrived and was ushered to the same table. Ralph introduced him formally to Zoe. They sat down. Ralph's guests looked a little puzzled, unsure why they had been invited.

"There should have been five of us," Ralph explained. "This is by way of being a celebration, a celebration and a thank you meal."

"Thank you?" Arthur was especially puzzled.

"The fifth guest should have been Gordon Scrimshaw. He's my accountant and he has helped make me a lot of money. But I owe each of you a great deal, Chris, because you have stood by me all these months and years. There were times when I treated you shamefully and I apologise. You have kindly allowed me to stay in your flat for months. You have seen me recover from all my afflictions, including my curious behaviour both before and after my accident. I have no idea how you manage to put up with me. As for Zoe, you picked me up when I was in a very bad physical and mental state. I know other specialists at the hospital did their stuff, but mending a broken mind, as you have done, is remarkable. I'll never be able to thank you properly."

Chris and Zoe were looking uncomfortable.

"As for Mr Clarke, you probably have no idea what you have done for me."

"I thought it was the other way round," said Arthur. "You came along for a month and worked without pay as a labourer. You help me out of a hole."

"I enjoyed it. But, as I said, you probably have no idea what it is you have done for me. I said this was a celebration and, in a sense, that's because of you."

Arthur looked extremely puzzled by this.

"I told you one day that I could not understand how you remain so steadfast and almost happy when you had lost your wife. It's not as though it was an unhappy marriage, after all. I remembered it was you who gave me Colin's bicycle. Colin," he explained for the benefit of Zoe and Chris, "was their son. He was killed in the war. Arthur not only gave me his bike; he also began teaching me how to ride it."

Zoe and Chris smiled appreciatively.

"But it was more recently that you told me something which inspired me." Ralph was looking at Arthur who remained puzzled. "When I observed that you were – the only word is steadfast in the face of all your problems, with a farm to run single-handedly while still grieving for Dorothy. I remember Dorothy. She was kind, helpful, lovely, and you were a wonderful couple."

"What are you talking about, boy?"

"You quoted from the Bible," said Ralph, and he quoted in his turn, "To everything there is a season, and a time for everything under heaven; a time to be born and a time to die; a time to plant at a time to pluck the things which have been planted."

All three were now staring at him intently.

"You also pointed out that, as a farmer, you understood the importance of seasons. And that has helped me more than you can ever know. Death is part of life. In a way grief is like being unwilling to accept the inevitable. We have to learn to put the past where it belongs and to get on with the next stage, the next season."

Ralph's three guests remained unsure what he was talking about.

"Sorry to bore you all," he said. "I said this was a celebration. It's a celebration of several things at once, as well as being a way to say thank you. I think I have recovered my senses, though you may well question that. I'm sorry that Gordon could not be here because the money he has earned for me will certainly help me. I am about to 'pluck that which was planted'. I am cashing in my winnings on the Stock Exchange in order to spend the next three years in Dublin."

"Dublin? Why Dublin?" Chris asked.

"I have decided that I want to study archaeology."

"But why Dublin?"

"A large part of their undergraduate course concentrates on Irish archaeology. Ireland is still largely Celtic, it's the Celts I am interested in especially. My experiences on Deadman's Down have left me with an interest in the Celts."

Arthur, Chris, and Zoe stared at Ralph, not sure what to make of his decision. However, Chris and Zoe exchanged a meaningful glance.

"All well, good luck to you, boy," said Arthur. "I don't know what the connection is between Dublin and Sussex, but I dare say you can find one. I'm sure we'll all miss you."

"Thank you," said Ralph. "I imagine you'll be quite happy to get your flat back to yourself, Chris."

"I always said you are welcome to stay as long as you wanted."

"But?"

"This could be very good news for us," Zoe said." We have decided we want to set up a proper home together and neither my flat nor Chris's is really fit for purpose. There are some new houses being built quite close to the hospital, I'm sure you know. The problem is that we would need to sell up both flats to raise the money."

"You should have kicked me out earlier!"

"Don't be daft! I couldn't do that, not after all that you've been through. Your life a whole history of losses. Your father rejected you. I'm hardly likely to do the same, am I?"

"Well, it sounds as though I'm going at just the right time," said Ralph. "Here's a toast to your new life together and to my new life in Dublin."

"You might be interested," Arthur said as they set down their glasses, "to know that I have decided to move on as well."

"Move on?" Ralph was very surprised. "Don't tell me you're going to retire? What on earth would you do with yourself?"

"No, not exactly. I'm really getting too old to run the farm myself. You know, young Ralph, when you refused to stay on with your father, he was badly upset."

"Yes, I'm still sorry about that. I know he wanted to pass the farm onto me. I just did not want to be a farmer."

"I know. Colin"– he turned to Zoe and Chris – "Colin was our son. I expected him to take over from me, but it was not to be. Anyway," he said more briskly, "I have decided to look for a young couple to run the farm for me. There's a great shortage of opportunity for young people to get started in farming. The farmhouse is big enough for a young family and I'm going to move into one of my own cottages. I'll be around for advice, but it will be up to the youngsters to run the place. If it works, they can in time rent it from me. It will free me to travel a bit."

"What about your cottage?" Chris was looking at Ralph.

"You are quite right about that," Ralph conceded. "I must have been slightly mad and now, as you said at the time, I'm stuck with a white elephant. There is a very slight chance I could get some money back."

"No one is going to want to buy it, surely?"

"No, you're right about that. However, it seems there is a very small, niche market. One or two creative artists, not quite as mad as me, composers, painters, writers, sometimes look for somewhere extremely remote on a long term let. It will have to be advertised extremely discreetly, otherwise it will look like an open invitation to thieves or burglars or even, short-term squatters. It's a possibility."

"Oh dear," said Zoe, "it has been a costly mistake."

"True," Ralph agreed. "I shall probably need to make it much more burglar-proof, and I must write it off as a very expensive mistake."

"Look on the bright side," said Chris, "you could have ended up dead. No one will ever understand how you manage to get yourself down to the main road."

"Well, I'm all better now. I have a couple of pins in my ankle, otherwise I'm as fit as a fiddle."

"I think your idea," said Chris, speaking to Arthur, "is excellent. However, the young couple are who take over, they can count themselves very lucky. My

Congratulations to you. This really is a celebration, then!"

Postscript

Five years passed. Ralph Cobden drove a heavy duty, four-wheel-drive vehicle and turned off the road up the overgrown track. In the passenger seat Eileen clung on as the vehicle bucked and jolted its way.

"When you said it was off the beaten track," she said, "you weren't joking."

Ralph laughed as the vehicle rocked. Here and there along the track plants had grown up. The truck crushed them. Where there had once been bare chalk exposed on the edges of the track, now there were tall weeds and saplings, cutting out much of the view. They arrived at the entrance to the quarry.

"On foot now," Ralph said.

Very little could be seen of the quarry itself. Numerous trees grow to a height of ten or twelve feet. What chalk remained exposed was now green. They walked over the grass, which was also tall and rough, so they will glad to be wearing thick trousers, and they arrived at the flat area in which the cottage stood. Here, what had once been bare, chalky bedrock, had also been reclaimed by nature. There was a fine stand of fire weed. They push their way through this to arrive at the building. The sheets of wood bolted to the window frames and the doors were stained with algae. The gutters had been long since filled with rubbish so that rain ran over the top and down the walls. Even now it was possible to admire the workmanship of those who had laid the flints in the walls. The garage-like building which housed the generator had long since been emptied of its contents which had been salvaged.

"And you say," Eileen asked, "all the furniture and fittings are still inside?"

"Most of them. I rescued all the books and put them in storage. I have no use for most of the furniture."

"At some time in the future," Eileen said, "someone will come along and open this up. They'll find kind of time capsule. It seems such a waste to leave it here."

"I suppose so. A friend of mine described it as a white elephant. I doubt of the find another madman who will want to renovate it. All I know is I can't sell it. Anyway, this is not what we came to see."

They climbed to the short rise to the top of the Down. Eileen gazed down at the view of the Weald, but she was not allowed to wait for long before Ralph moved impatiently onward. The path along the crest of the Downs was quite clear, but he almost missed the turning which led down to Druids Wood. After several years he still had to brace himself to summon up the courage to enter. Inside, nothing had changed. The bough on which he had sat to drink his tea, pouring some of it as a libation to the ancient gods, was still in the same place, the silence was profound. He felt all his muscles tense and he was about to shiver.

"This place is creepy," Eileen said. "I don't want to stay in here."

Outside, under the autumn sky, they hugged for mutual comfort before retracing their steps. It was only when they were inside the cab of the vehicle and had slammed the doors that the sombre mood lifted a little.

"Let's get out of here," Eileen said.

"You have to admit," Ralph said as he wrestled with the steering wheel, "there is something very strange about that place."

"I'm not surprised you haven't been back."

"' A time to kill and a time to heal'" said Ralph.

"What?"

"A quotation."

"Oh! Can we find somewhere for a cup of tea? For some reason I'm cold." And they headed for the bright, bustling warmth of town.

THE END

Other titles by Ian Searle

Mary Field, 58, and her academic husband, Greg, are about to leave Australia for a lengthy holiday in Europe, when Mary learns she has inherited a property in England. It belonged to a distant relative. The couple discover Judge Lucien Malpas was murdered at the age of 95.

Before they finally track down the killer, they form close relationships and lasting friendships in the community in which they find themselves. For Mary especially the experience is both challenging and life-changin.

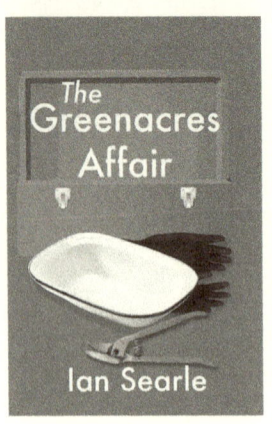

Gordon Drake has no time properly to take up his post at Greenacres School in the summer of 1960. A suspicious death produces chaos among the staff, who have all been recalled during the long holiday.

Someone at the school is responsible for the death, and the ensuing police investigation is not only a threat to the very existence of the school, but uncovers both negligent school governors as well as fraud. The community faces an uncertain future.

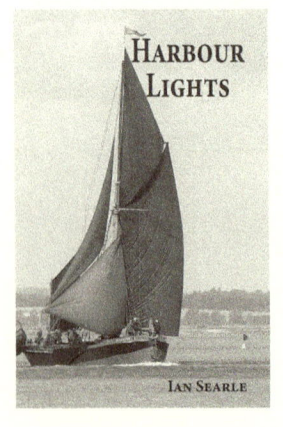

It's not every day that your father presents you with a tumbledown building and the funds to convert it into a hotel. It's not every day, either, that you learn his financial empire was built on theft.

That is what happens to Tom Hammond. He takes on the challenge but it soon goes wrong. The struggle to survive and succeed threatens to defeat him. The experience affects his health and forces fundamental changes in his personal relationship.